The Gift

by

Jon Kalb

The Gift

Copyright 2007

by

Jon Kalb

Cover design by Bill Montgomery and Jack Moore

ISBN

1-934335-06-1

978-1-934335-06-2

Special Delivery Books

46561 State Highway 118

Alpine, TX 79830

Dedicated to
Peter Kalb

Prologue

Morlock

A pale light seeped from beneath the closed door and voices filtered down the hallway into his room. Another meeting. Right now he pictured his mother smiling while serving tea and homemade cookies, chocolate macaroons, his favorite. Earlier she gave him "two and only two," like he was a *kid*.

After his father asked him to greet everyone, he was sent to bed. He hated that. Not that he wanted to sit around listening to "God this" and "God that." He liked to hear them argue and watch them get red in the face, while talking about other people in the church.

Really stupid was "lights out" at nine o'clock. But tonight he didn't care. Elsie, his two-year-old sister, slept in the next room. Everybody thought she was so darling, like he didn't exist. Toys covered the floor of her room, as if she needed them all, and books lined her shelves, as if she could read them. Right now he was reading *The Time Machine* by H. G. Wells for the fourth time.

His mother said it was "unnatural for a seven-year-old to read adult books, especially the same one over and over again."

But he loved it, to be a meat-eating Morlock and kill the soft and weak Eloi. He wanted to do that. He wanted to smash their heads in, eat their brains, and then dance around a bonfire.

Bertie knew the meeting would drag on another hour. Then everyone would pray and go home. He had just heard his mother go into Elsie's room to make sure her precious daughter was warm and cuddly. After a few minutes, she returned to the living room. He waited awhile longer, picked up his pillow, and ran to the door. He slowly opened it. He could clearly hear their conversation.

"It seems to me," said one, "that we've done enough for the homeless. We have to draw the line!"

"I agree," said another. "We need to do more for our own home. We need a new roof, the organ needs repair, and the . . ."

Who cares, thought Bertie. He looked up and down the hall. Empty. He dashed into Elsie's room, like a Morlock hunting at night. He closed the door. The glow of the streetlight from the window illuminated his sister asleep in her crib. He was big for his age. It would be easy. He grabbed his pillow with both hands.

That night he slept well, despite his mother's screams that later filled the house. Bertie dreamed he was a great warrior dancing around a bonfire.

Chapter 1

A Precocious Son

Bert Wilde was born in 1950 in Austin, Texas, the son of a Methodist minister with a devoted following and a devoted wife. His parents knew he was special, but they worried about his emotional development. He interacted well with adults, but treated children as inferiors and had no regular playmates. With that in mind, his parents sent him to St. Stephens, an expensive private school, reasoning that the financial sacrifice would be worth the extra social instruction he received.

Accustomed to being the center of attention, Bert was not pleased when a baby sister joined him. But she died mysteriously in her sleep. The family doctor attributed the tragedy to Sudden Infant Death Syndrome. Bert's mother wasn't so sure and harbored a deep, unspoken suspicion of her son, which did not lessen as he grew older.

Drawing on his great size, even in elementary school, Bert bullied the boys in his classes and developed a reputation among the girls as an over-attentive tease. His teachers warned one another that Bert needed to be "watched." On the other hand, his high school record proved his exceptional intellect. The lowest grade he received in four years was a single B in Honors English from Miss Motley, a frail, gray-haired teacher. However, when he confronted her in her office after school, his size and demeanor were so threatening that she reconsidered her decision.

"But Miss *Molty*," Bert hissed at her, while sitting on the edge of her desk staring into her face, "the B grade may suit you but it does not suit me, so please rethink your decision."

She raised his grade to an A.

By the end of his senior year, Bert stood at six-feet-four inches tall and weighed 250 pounds, most of it muscle from power lifting, the only physical exercise he pursued, mainly because it made the girls more interested in him than they already were. Despite his rugged good looks, his classmates called him "The Red Beast," both for his size and his shaggy red hair.

He continued to bully the boys and made it a point of letting every girl he dated know that he carried condoms, although he seldom took the trouble to use them. The girls knew he was "physical" on dates, and at least one of his conquests became pregnant. Fortunately, she dropped out of school and he never saw her again.

By age 26, Wilde had completed both his undergraduate and doctoral degrees in anthropology at the University of Chicago. His area of interest was paleoanthropology, particularly the search for the fossil remains of our earliest ancestors in Africa. When asked how he became interested in human origins, he said he believed it came from listening to his father's sermons about the Book of Genesis and the notion that God made man in his own image on the fifth day. Even as a youngster, he considered the idea a fanciful myth to be challenged.

While at Chicago, Bert joined three expeditions in Africa, although he found the climate and camping distasteful. Instead, he preferred to usurp the discoveries of his fellow students in subtle, or not so subtle ways. In addition to the senior scientists on the team, the expeditions included both male and female graduate students. At the beginning of each field season Bert always proclaimed which female team member was best suited to be "Bert's Slut of the Month."

By the time he completed his doctorate, with honors, in 1977, he had published a dozen scientific papers on human evolution in international journals. His professors anticipated that he would have a brilliant career.

After Chicago, Bert was snapped up by Rice University, where he barreled through the academic ranks, becoming a full professor at age 29. He continued fieldwork in East Africa, making a respectable showing of fossil finds, but nothing spectacular. Rather, among his peers he was best known for his lengthy and incisive publications reinterpreting the discoveries of others. During his years at Rice, he was also known as a ladies' man, both among the faculty and with his more discreet graduate students.

A turning point in Professor Wilde's career came in 1985 when he married Alice Masterson, a tall brunette studying art history. An unobtrusive person with pleasant features, she signed up for Wilde's introductory course on human evolution on a lark and soon became fascinated with paleoanthropology. Rather, she became infatuated with

Wilde. His handsome yet brutish looks and his flirtatious manner and gossipy humor about his colleagues were a combination she found oddly appealing and sexual.

Late one fall afternoon he offered Alice a ride home, which she readily accepted, although she lived nearby. Wilde was overwhelmed by her "graduate student housing," a magnificent Tudor-style mansion on Remington Lane just north of the university in one of Houston's oldest and most fashionable neighborhoods.

When Wilde learned that Alice's parents had died in a car crash several months earlier, and that she had no siblings, he decided on the spot that this was the person he would marry. He became a regular visitor on Remington Lane and Alice came to idolize "Bertie."

She felt flattered by the attention he gave her and grateful for the caring she needed at that stage in her life. Unfortunately, his regard for her, aside from her bedroom enthusiasm, was more practicable in nature. Creating a scandal on the small Rice campus, where faculty was certainly not expected to be intimate with students, the two were married that December. They set the date soon after her parents' wills were probated, and it was clear that Alice was a girl of considerable wealth. Following a three-day honeymoon in the Bahamas, Bert moved into the Remington home and sold his condo next to the football stadium.

Chapter 2

Equus antiguas

Ron Slater picked his way along a steep gravel embankment. Suddenly, the cobbles beneath his feet shot forward like billiard balls sending him tumbling and crashing down the steep slope of a ravine covered with catclaw and mesquite. He landed on his back with a shattering jolt.

"Son of a bitch!" He grimaced.

Slater's 170-pound frame was punctured, scraped, and scratched from his boot tops to the top of his head. Blood oozed through his thick black hair and trickled down the back of his neck. He had just fallen into the Scorpion Arroyo on the eastern flank of the Rio Grande Valley in the southeastern Chihuahuan Desert.

As the vulture flies, he lay sprawled sixteen miles northwest of the town of Presidio, in the county of the same name. Not so high in the sky, vultures started to circle. Suddenly, one cocked its wings and banked into a hasty turn to a lower level.

"Screw you," Slater croaked. "I'm not dead . . . yet."

The vulture, unimpressed, continued to drop for a closer look.

Slater groaned and rolled gingerly onto his left side. Propping himself up on his elbow, he slipped out of his daypack and quickly took an inventory: arms, legs, fingers, toes, ribs, and skull. Nope, nothing broken; nothing needed stitches. The cut on his scalp was minor.

Before he moved, however, he pulled out his pocketknife and spent ten minutes removing the more accessible thorns and needles from his limbs and torso. Then he rolled over to his right side and repeated the process. Later, he would bathe at the nearby Chinati hot springs to help soak out the more minute spines. If that didn't work, he would have to shave them off.

"Ronald, my boy, you're an idiot," was heard by whatever creatures lurked about. The vultures, realizing they would have to wait for another day for this one, slipped into a thermal and leisurely lifted off.

Slowly he stood up and peeled his torn and bloodied shirt off his back and laid it out on some rocks to dry. Of average height, lean and muscular, Slater was accustomed to desert terrain and its pitfalls, having spent much of his youth exploring his home state of Arizona. He wasn't handsome, but women found his deep-set hazel eyes, strong features, and poorly repaired broken nose appealing.

He opened his pack, pulled out a sheepskin water bag and took a couple of gulps. He looked at his watch, which fortunately had survived the fall.

"Damn, already 11:00." He guessed it was already 105 degrees.

"Another hot one, boys," he said to a pair of lizards scurrying nearby. "Better find some shade."

He knew that by 4:00 p.m. the temperature would

hover between 112 and 116 degrees, as it had been for the past two weeks. At 10:00 p.m. it would still be in the low nineties.

The calendar on his watch read July 16, the hottest month of the year on the border, made hotter still by eight years of drought. Many desert plants, including cacti, acacias, and even mesquite, had dried up leaving nothing living in their place to absorb the heat.

He dusted himself off and looked up the embankment for his prize cowboy hat that he had recently purchased from the Trans-Pecos Saddlery in Alpine. Imported from Guatemala, it was well-suited to the pounding West Texas sun. Its tough, tightly woven straw and extra wide brim also had a tie cord with a slipknot under the chin to keep it from flying off when the fiery, dry winds raced across the Rio Grande Valley floor. To his chagrin, Slater found the hat impaled on a dagger yucca. Still dazed from his fall, he stumbled over to retrieve it when something white caught his eye a few feet ahead. Not a stream pebble. He picked it up.

"Whoa! A horse molar and definitely not recent," he murmured. "Fossil."

He pulled out his knife from the scabbard on his hip and scratched away some sand lightly cemented to the square-shaped crown.

"Yes, the enamel pattern is *Equus,*" he continued. "Definitely not a modern species. Too small for one thing, but not a juvenile. Heavily worn. An adult. But not battered by stream wash, meaning the tooth had recently eroded out of a sediment layer. Which layer?"

Slater spit on the crown and wiped it off on his jeans.

He turned the tooth over and over.

"It has to be *Equus antiguas*, the smaller horse that roamed the Southwest several million years ago."

Just what he was looking for. This equid and a handful of other mammalian fossils were reported from "Scorpion Arroyo, 15 mi NW of Presidio town" in an obscure, unpublished report written in 1936 by Lowell Dudley, a geologist employed by the Texas Bureau of Economic Geology in Austin. The director of the Bureau at the time, Ellias Schafer, had a special interest in vertebrate paleontology, especially "early man." As a result, he authorized wide-ranging fossil and archeological surveys throughout the state in cooperation with Depression-era public work projects.

Apparently, because of the paucity of the Scorpion Arroyo find, the fossils attracted little attention and drew dust in one storage room or another at the Bureau for the next 61 years. In 1997, they were rediscovered and handed over to the Vertebrate Paleontology Laboratory, known as the VP Lab for short. Both buildings were part of the research complex belonging to the University of Texas in north Austin. It was at the laboratory in late June of the following year that Slater came across the Dudley collection. He worked there as a technical assistant conscripted from the Anthropology Department's work-study program, made possible by the good graces of his Ph.D. supervisor: Professor Bert Wilde.

Chapter 3

Alice's Endowment

Wilde's marriage to Alice proved to be the windfall he anticipated, providing him with a sizable discretionary budget. Fortunately for him, her parents left their fortune to their only child directly, not impinged by trusts. Soon, Wilde's research credits began to increase substantially. In Africa, he began exercising his influence with compliant officials who gave him enormous concessions to the richest fossil areas and in the process, claim-jumped areas found by others.

As a result, Wilde's team made a succession of important discoveries, including fossil hominids several million years older than the oldest found by the Leakey family, and one million years older than the three-million-year-old "Lucy" skeleton found in Ethiopia in 1974.

Wilde's success in Africa was made all the more possible back home by select officials of the U.S. National Science Foundation, who—with certain incentives—made sure his grant applications were approved over others, by-passing NSF's renowned peer review system.

As far as Alice's marriage went, her husband paid less and less attention to her as time went by. His absences from home grew longer and longer, despite promises that things would get better the next semester, then the next, and the next. She dropped out of graduate studies because Bert felt marriage to a student tarnished his image. That left her with volunteer work at the nearby Contemporary Art Museum, which soon bored her, as did most dinners she prepared for distinguished guests, who could advance Bert's ambitions.

She fell into depression and desperately wanted children, but "noise" was the last thing Bert wanted while at home.

"Just keep going to teas and look charming," he told her. "That would be of great help." That she did, but with no close family to turn to and most of her friends raising children or pursuing careers, she soon replaced tea with wine, then wine for vodka, and by their sixth year of marriage, she was a closet alcoholic.

In 1993, Wilde made a sensational find: a largely complete skeleton of a chimpanzee-like hominid, a prize sought by paleoanthropologists for three decades. In the 1960s, molecular studies had predicted—based on rates of gene mutations—that the divergence of the earliest hominids from the great apes took place four to six million years ago. Of the African great apes, the chimpanzees share the most genes with humans and are considered our closest relatives.

The human ancestor discovered by Wilde shared many features with chimps. A major distinction, however, was that it had walked on two legs, a feature long believed to be unique to humans. As a bipedal ape, or an ape-like human, the discovery filled a major gap in the ape-human transition. Radiometric dating, based on the rate of decay of naturally occurring radioactive elements, placed its age at five million years, right on target with the prediction of molecular biologists. The discovery appeared on the covers of *Nature* and *Time* magazines and turned Professor Wilde into a talk-show celebrity.

The following year, 1994, the distinguished fossil hunter accepted a professorship at Harvard University, and two years later, was elected to the U.S. National Academy of Sciences. With his career at its peak, however, "some spineless scumbag" exposed NSF's more confidential funding practices to its Inspector General. Charges of "grant-fixing" detailed exactly how Wilde received an $850,000 grant for continued work in Africa, the year of his "fabulous find."

The award was intended to fund four field seasons and complementary laboratory work. As a result of the charges, however, Wilde's grant funds drained to a trickle, he was quietly booted out of Harvard, and his membership in the National Academy of Sciences hung in the balance. To top it off, his latest fossil concession in Africa was seized by rivals who despised him.

Now out of a job and desperate to avoid public disgrace, Wilde dropped hints to influential people in Austin that he, and especially his "long-suffering wife," yearned to return to Texas. Both he and Alice, he declared, were unhappy in the rarefied atmosphere of Cambridge. One conversation led to another, and soon Wilde was offered a chaired professorship at the University of Texas, a position he grabbed. As the only member of the Anthropology Department elected to the National Academy of Sciences—and unaware of Wilde's reversals at NSF and

Harvard—the university was delighted to have won such a prize, a hometown boy at that. His father was now pastor of Austin's largest Methodist church. Sadly, his mother died of cancer a few years earlier, when Bert was away in Africa. To her last breath she believed her son had murdered her beloved Elsie.

ψψψ

Ron Slater was at the end of his third year at Harvard when the bottom dropped out of his career and especially his personal life. He was well into his dissertation research on a site in East Africa when Professor Wilde abruptly left Harvard for Texas, for reasons few understood outside of the offices of the Harvard president and its general counsel. With his usual bravado, Wilde told people that his fellow Texans made him an offer no sane man could refuse. He assured Slater, however, that he could continue working with his team in Africa to complete his field research for his doctorate. But shortly after Wilde left for Austin, word circulated that he had lost his rich fossil concession in Africa.

Like others, Slater assumed the loss was connected to the cutthroat territorial competition for fossils between scientific teams. Regardless, this left Slater and a half-dozen other graduate students scrambling for new dissertation projects, and ways to overcome months of lost time and scholarship money. But all of this paled compared to the tragedy in his private life.

In early June, Slater's fellow student, and fiancée, Laura Hudson, died of complications from an abortion when she was two months pregnant. Slater was devastated and inconsolable. He had no idea she was pregnant and he was incredulous that she had not told him. They had even talked about having children. He knew Laura was upset about something toward the end of the spring semester, but she led him to believe it concerned her heavy course load. He was too immersed in work to notice anything more serious. She died just before her 26th birthday. A wholesome, direct person who was raised on a dairy farm in Montana by very religious parents, she had mahogany-colored hair and pale green eyes.

During her high school years, she proved to be a true scholar in the making. In some ways, her rural upbringing led her to be naive to the ways of the world. She accepted people at face value and trusted them to a fault, something she and Slater had argued about. As fellow students, the two of them had come to know and love each other during two field seasons in Africa, with a third season together planned for the fall. They had much in common in their scientific interests, and shared a love of outdoor life. Slater was crushed, even mystified, by her death.

None of it made sense, and his grief and guilt knew no end. Even while attending her funeral in Montana, he knew something was missing, but there was nothing to be gained from talking to her family and friends since they clearly held him responsible for her death.

CBCBCB

To pick up the pieces of the career that Laura had expected of him, Slater decided to follow Wilde to the

University of Texas and enroll in its anthropology program. He hoped that a change of environments would help heal his sorrow and torment. Slater didn't care for Wilde's vaulted ego, or his relentless muckraking remarks about his rivals, but he did offer to arrange financial support for Slater if he transferred to Texas, which he did.

Slater had been one of Wilde's top students in the classroom and was equally competent in the field. Also, for three years he had worked as his technical assistant in Harvard's acclaimed Museum of Comparative Zoology, where he was considered the best student preparator of fossils the museum had seen in years. His steady hands and patience while removing rock matrix from fossils with an air scribe or dental picks were first-rate, as were his reconstructions. For museum exhibits, his preparation of casts of fossils were so genuine in appearance that on several occasions his reproductions were confused with the originals.

As part of his emotional recovery in Texas, Slater plunged into a new dissertation project, one involving fieldwork that could somehow tie in with his now-abandoned research in Africa. His fellow students were impressed by his long work hours, but found him withdrawn and a loner, which they attributed to his "Harvardness."

He became intrigued with the Rio Grande Valley in far West Texas when he learned that it was a rift valley similar to that in eastern Africa. Both were linear depressions formed by the incremental separation of the earth's crust. Faulting and erosion exposed the rift margins while the floors of the rifts accumulated sediments thousands of feet

16

thick. In the African rift, such processes have buried and preserved the fossil and cultural remains of our earliest ancestors dating back millions of years. Slater knew that the Rio Grande rift was not another "cradle of humankind," but its sediments were deeply eroded and its low rainfall favored the preservation of fossils once they were exposed to the surface.

ೞೞೞ

Slater accepted the fossil evidence that humans, the genus *Homo*, originated in Africa at least 2.5 million years ago, then crossed into Eurasia 800,000 years or more later. He also thought it plausible that humans began migrating into North America during the last ice age, beginning some 20,000 years ago, perhaps using boats, as archeologists increasingly believe. The most accepted explanation for the appearance of Paleoindians in the New World proposes that they walked across a land bridge connecting Siberia with Alaska. This was made possible during a period of decreased global temperatures and a fall of sea levels, turning the Bering Strait into a dry landmass, named Beringia.

Archeological evidence indicates that immigrants reached North America no later than 11,500 years ago, and then moved southward seeking new territories at the rate of 50 miles per year—in the blink of time, geologically—like beads of mercury spilling across a tabletop. These colonists, the "first Americans," were accomplished big game hunters, as indicated by their distinctive fluted projectile points first found lodged in the skeletons of mammoths in Clovis, New Mexico.

When Slater decided to look for fossils in the Rio Grande Valley, starting with the Scorpion Arroyo, he was on familiar ground, in that rift valleys and deserts halfway around the world from each other share common features, including unique prehistories of human origins. Surprisingly, other than Dudley's sparse collection, few mammalian fossils had been documented in the Presidio County part of the rift, nor had artifacts been found as old as Clovis.

Although Slater's interest in early humans was more in the millions-of-years range, he would be delighted to find paleofaunas in the Rio Grande Valley similar in age (early Pleistocene) to those he had found in Africa—between one and two million years—even though he knew that the recovery of human fossil and cultural remains of this time period in Texas was out of the question. Such a comparison of animals from the two continents could, however, offer insights on the relative effects of hunting on animal populations in the early Pleistocene (in Africa), or its absence during this same period (in North America). The prospect of finding a Clovis, or pre-Clovis, site left by prehistoric American hunters to contrast with Early Stone Age sites left by African hunters was also enticing, even though the two groups were separated in time by at least one-and-a-half million years.

Chapter 4

Scorpion Arroyo

Satisfied that he was in one piece after his dive into the arroyo, Slater picked up his shredded shirt, now encrusted with dried blood and sweat, and gingerly slipped it on along with his daypack. He found his geology pick where he dropped it and began searching the dry streambed for more fossils. Among the gravels, he found a few unidentifiable bone fragments, but fossils nonetheless.

"They must have come from a nearby source," he reasoned. "Certainly not the thick alluvial gravels that capped the overlying plateau, which came from a distant high energy source. The breaks on the fossils were too pristine, like the Dudley fossils back at the VP Lab, to have been transported by the same floods that deposited the gravels over the millennia.

"Yes, these fossils are the product of lower energy deposition that buried dead animals beside the likes of a slow meandering stream."

He walked slowly up the arroyo. After a few minutes he found a layer of sandstone protruding from the bank beneath the gravels. Chunks of sandstone lay below. Using his pick he gently scraped away the loose gravel from above. As he did, he exposed a much thicker sandstone layer, interbedded with silts and clays.

But after further exposing the sandstone with his pick, he found nothing more than a single leg bone fragment of an antelope. Nevertheless, he figured he was hot on the trail of more fossils and it wouldn't take him long.

Wrong.

Throughout the rest of July and much of August, Slater combed Scorpion Arroyo and a dozen other drainages, as the daytime temperature continued to hover in the triple digits. The only cool times of the day were between first light and the first few hours after the sun ascended over the Chinati Mountains to the east, and in the late afternoon after the sun slipped behind Sierra Caliente in Mexico.

Frequently dark clouds formed in the late afternoon, teasingly suggesting a rainstorm, but usually resulted in a fleeting cool spell, sometimes followed by a swift dust storm and "dry" lightning. A few drops of rain might follow. The local joke described such precipitation in terms of inches of rain, the distance from one raindrop to the next. A real rain shower typically vaporized before it hit ground or was instantaneously sucked into the scorched earth.

The area Slater surveyed lay southeast of the Chinati hot springs, where he kept his camp. Surrounded by high cottonwood trees, the lithium-rich springs were remote, privately owned, and maintained with a water temperature of 109 degrees year-round.

Camping areas, four small cabins, and a small kitchen were available for modest fees. All were managed by a brother and a sister, Fernando and Rocío Benavides. They worked at the springs during the summer months at no salary in exchange for free room and board. They attended college the rest of the year. Because of a long-time financial arrangement between their parents, Fernando was an American citizen raised by their father in Presidio, and Rocío was Mexican raised by their mother in San Antonio del Bravo, a small village across the Rio Grande not far from the springs. A two-foot-wide iron footbridge spanning the river united the village with Candelaria, an even smaller settlement on the U.S. side of the border. During holidays the family got together as though never separated.

Over the summer, Slater came to admire Fernando and Rocío. Fernando attended Sul Ross State College in nearby Alpine and studied engineering; Rocío studied biology at Chihuahua University in Ciudad Chihuahua, a three-hour drive from Presidio. Their parents, Enrique and Rosie, were high school teachers whose respective families had lived in the area for generations. According to Enrique, it was likely their families stretched back 10,000 years to the Jumano Indians, said to be the earliest agriculturalists in North America.

When not cleaning out the large tiled tubs at the springs used by the guests, Fernando was frequently off by himself reading at a picnic table beneath a cottonwood tree. Big and broad shouldered, he usually went around camp wearing shorts, a T-shirt, sandals, and a baseball cap. Rocío dressed similarly while at the springs, but more often she was off exploring the arroyos, wearing patched-up jeans, a long sleeve shirt, a cowboy hat with the rim turned down, and hiking boots that looked like they had been dropped into a food processor. She maintained the grounds of the springs and was gregarious and talkative with visitors, who were pleased to hear her explanations of the natural history of the area, which she amended from day to day with each new discovery. She could identify a multitude of birds; the tracks, droppings, and lairs of animals; more snakes than she cared to know; and the names of plants that were edible or useful for medicinal purposes by *curanderos*. Rocío's father called her the Apache of the family, characterized by her long gait, her ability to spend hours in the countryside without water, and her classic *mestizo* features: high cheekbones, firm muscles, long black hair tied in a pony tail, and the golden glow of her skin. In fact, like most Mexicans, she was large part Indian and some part Spanish.

The local ranchers came to know Rocío and expect her exploration forays across their property, fences or no fences, and recognized her for the hummingbird she was. On occasion new Border Patrol recruits in their green and white Chevy SUVs—called *perreras*, or "dog catchers," by the border Mexicans—spotted her crossing a dirt road, or off in the hills, and made the mistake of trying to chase her down, only to see her vanish into the brush like a puff of dust.

∞∞∞

Slater's quest for extinct animals fascinated Rocío, and she barraged him with questions when he returned to camp in the late afternoons, seemingly not waiting to hear his answer to one question before she asked him another one.

"Ronaldo, why did the *animales* became extinct?"

"*Por qué* you find the *fosíles* on one side of the *río* and not the other?"

"Why did they become into rock?"

And so on. Slater could not help but be attracted to this inquisitive creature, who seemed to be a part of nature like everything else. Her earnest and open manner reminded him of his past relationship with Laura, causing him to brusquely ignore Rocío's constant requests to take her with him during her free time.

"It's too dangerous," he told her grabbing at any excuse.

"It's too what?" she laughed.

"Dangerous."

"Too *peligroso*?" she said, "I'm not believing my ears! Surely you're making joke with me, Ronaldo. You're the one coming back to *campo* looking like chopped *chorizo*!"

"One time, that happened just one time," he protested. It was Rocío who pulled the remaining thorns and needles out of Slater's back after his fall into the arroyo.

"In fact, Ronaldo, don't forget who pulled all those thorns and needles out of your back *porque tú no sabes* the difference between catclaw, cactus, and the creosote bush."

Slater did agree to take her to see some fossils, if he ever found anything worthy.

CBCBCB

Typically, Slater took his much-abused Ford pickup with him at sunrise and parked it out of view on one of the gravel roads leading into the hinterlands. The area he selected to survey for fossils, surrounding Scorpion Arroyo, lay on a 32,000-acre ranch owned jointly by twin brothers, Roper and Rider Harrington. It was Roper who ran the ranch, while Rider ran the family hardware store in nearby Marfa. The land was originally part of a 228,000-acre ranch owned by their great-grandfather, Captain Jacob Harrington, who served in the Texas Brigade under General John Bell Hood during the Civil War. Both men were severely wounded during the war. Hood, twice shot from his horse, lost his left leg at Chikamauga and use of his left hand at Gettysburg. Harrington was bayoneted in the face and neck at Antietam. But they survived the slaughter, married, and raised large families.

Hood became a merchant in New Orleans, while Harrington took a gamble and bought a dozen silver prospects in the Chinati Mountains, now part of a resort ranch called Cebolo Ranch. For capital, he used money from the sale of 500 acres of black cotton farmland he inherited just west of Houston. Both his father and grandfather had been successful farmers, but after fighting his way back and forth across the South during the war, the captain wanted to keep as much space around him as possible and chose to raise cattle, not grow cotton.

As risk taking would have it, one of the silver prospects paid off handsomely in the upper Cibolo Creek area northwest of Presidio. With his profits, in 1875 Harrington bought land north and west of Presidio (at ten cents an acre) from the great-grandfather of Enrique Benavides, the father of Rocío and Fernando. The land included a slice of the Chinati Mountains. However, the acquisition proved of little immediate value since the highlands were traditionally the stronghold of the Mescalero Apaches, who periodically swept across the plains spreading havoc and shopping for whatever was on their grocery list: horses, cattle, scalps, women. This changed, however, in the 1880s when the U.S. Army built forts in the region. By then, the Comanches, along with the Apaches and Kiowa, had been decimated by the Texas Rangers and groups of vigilantes.

CXCXCX

Captain Harrington's Double-H Ranch, the name honoring his service under Hood, extended from Presidio to as far west as the Chinati springs and the nearby village of Ruidosa. In 1916, Ruidosa became one of eleven U.S. Army outposts built along the border to combat raids on Texas ranches by Pancho Villa during the Mexican Revolution. Today Ruidosa is reduced to a cantina, the haunting shell of a large, majestic adobe church filled with graffiti and bird droppings, and a small general store owned by Enrique Benavides. An attendant keeps the store open five days a week. Enrique visits on Saturdays bringing what supplies are needed from the Baeza's Supermarket in Presidio, then drives over to the springs to see his son and daughter and soak in the thermal waters. During the week he teaches history and English at Presidio High School. Enrique also serves as the resident historian of the area. One of his favorite topics of conversation is the pending "re-conquest"—when the higher birth rate of Mexican-Americans in Texas will eventually draw more Hispanics to the polls than Anglos.

CXCXCX

From the Rio Grande, the Double-H Ranch reaches as far north as the now abandoned Cibolo Silver Mine on Cibolo Creek. The profits from the mine brought several generations of Harringtons a measure of wealth until the silver played out in 1953. Over the years, most of the original Double-H Ranch was subdivided among the sons of one Harrington or another and sold off.

Roper Harrington gladly gave Slater permission to look for fossils on this ranch, as his father had done for Lowell Dudley in 1936.

"Son, this ranch *is* a fossil. If you want to look for petrified animals and you can take the heat, that's fine with me. Just leave any gates you go through like you found 'em and let me know if you find anything fit to feed cattle that I may not know about."

Slater agreed, but by the end of August he was spent. His only rewards were the horse tooth and the antelope limb bone. As one last effort, he went back to Scorpion Arroyo. He stood in the middle of the streambed and looked again at the sandstone exposure. His eyes followed the layer downstream until it disappeared beneath thick gravel. Then he turned around and followed it upstream as he had done before. Once again, the sandstone layer dropped out of sight. He noticed that it lay flush against layers of gravel.

"Son of a bitch!" he yelled, flushing a pair of warblers out of a nearby juniper tree. "I've been walking back and forth across a set of reverse faults!"

Rift valleys are typically bound by blocks of strata downthrown into the rift, along "normal" faults. Rare were "reverse" faults that left fault blocks elevated relative to surrounding strata. Such blocks were overlain by less overburden, such as gravels, than normal fault blocks simply because of their higher position. Slater slowly walked down the arroyo keeping his eyes glued to the banks alternately looking from one side to the other.

He stopped.

At the top of the right bank, he spotted patches of brown sandstone hidden behind agarita and clusters of thorn scrub. He walked closer, probed some bushes with a *sotol* stalk to flush out any rattlesnakes, then took a better look at the sandstone. Instead of massive overlying gravel like he had found further down the arroyo, there were only a few feet of overburden.

He looked carefully in the streambed and saw small clumps of coarse sandstone and . . . fossil bone? Down on his hands and knees he saw numerous small fragments of bone in between cobbles of quartz, volcanic rock, and limestone brought down from the Chinati Mountains. He guessed that the fossils eroded out of the sands in the stream banks and then fell into the arroyo, where they were all but obliterated by cattle moving from one grazing area or water source to another. The surface of the streambed was disturbed and worn slick by their tracks, amid abundant droppings. He guessed Dudley must have been lucky and happened on fossils eroded from a collapsed stream bank, perhaps brought on by a rainstorm.

Slater climbed up onto the plateau and spent the rest of the day dragging the blade of his pick back and forth, removing gravel until he reached the sandstone. He kept at it until he had exposed about twelve square feet of sand and poorly cemented sandstone, which he then excavated down another eighteen inches. By sundown, he had found several carnivore teeth, a partial bovid skull, a pig maxilla, a horn core of an antelope, and assorted post-cranial bones. He had struck pay dirt: a bone bed! Such concentrations of animal remains formed in the past, as today, when carcasses are typically swept up by flash floods.

Over the next five days, using a larger pick and a shovel borrowed from Roper, Slater steadily cleared away four sixteen-square-foot patches of gravel spaced out on the plateau next to the arroyo, demonstrating that the bone bed was not an isolated occurrence, but extensive. When he neared the top of the sandstone layer with his digging, he cleared away the rest of the overburden with a small pick and then by hand. Using a hunting knife and a whisk broom, he slowly removed the sand exposing whole and broken fossils, adding to the list of taxa he had found the previous day, including teeth and bones of camel and elk.

At least we have enough fossils to date them, he thought.

He also found molars of two species of equids, the smaller *Equus antiguas*, and a larger, more-evolved species. From his study of the Dudley collection, he knew that *antiguas* lived from about 3.0 to 1.5 million years, and the larger species lived from 1.8 million until the widespread extinctions at the end of the Ice Age, 10,000 years ago. The co-occurrence of the two horses between 1.8 and 1.5 million years greatly refined the age of the Scorpion Arroyo fossils to a 300,000 years interval.

In similar fashion, after Slater increased the list of identifiable taxa and compared their individual time ranges, he would be able to refine the age of the paleofauna further.

Ideally, he hoped to use radiometric dating to determine an even more accurate age of the fossils, but that would require finding volcanic materials for dating, and so far he had found none in or near the fossil-bearing layer.

Slater spent two more days at the arroyo photographing fossils, drawing stratigraphic sections, and making locality maps of the area. He left the larger and more fragile fossils buried and covered the excavated plots with brush, taking with him only a sample of what he hoped would be a considerable collection.

When Slater later showed the fossils to Roper, a man with hands the texture of a cedar post, the rancher picked out the horse and elk teeth right away and concluded, "Fella, if all you gotta do to become a scientist is to find old horse teeth and deer bones, then the next time I visit Austin, I want you to sign me up."

"Consider it done," said Slater. "At the very least come by the VP Lab and I'll give you a tour."

The two shook hands and Slater thanked him for his hospitality.

On his last day, Slater finally took Rocío with him to see the site, where she found some turtle bones right away. She was overwhelmed.

"See, Ronaldo, I should have helped you *todos los tiempos*. See how easy I find things. You should be ashamed of yourself! Next summer I will join you and that's a fact, *¿sí* ?"

"Well, I'll have to think about. . . "

"Think nothing! I study *zoología* at the *universidad*, and I know much about *animales*. These *fósiles* are not that different from the living *animales*, and I bet you did not know that."

Slater, unable to resist her taunting, smiled, "Okay, why not. But I also plan on returning for part of the Christmas holidays, for a week or so, and I was going to suggest that . . ."

"I join you?"

"Yes, well, for a few days if you . . ."

"You will camp at the hot springs?"

"Yes, for a day or so . . ."

"*Bueno*, my spies will tell me when you come."

Chapter 5

Rumors

Over the next few months Slater divided his time between the VP Lab and two graduate seminars on the main campus. Both courses, one under Wilde, the other under Craig Russell, also a paleoanthropologist, amounted to independent study projects requiring only a research paper at the end of the semester.

The project under Wilde was a routine literature search gathering the latest information on faunal migrations between Asia and North America during the Pleistocene, when sea levels fell as the ice caps thickened and glaciers moved southward. The project focused on dates when Paleoindians could have first reached North America. Wilde really didn't care when humans migrated from Asia 10,000, 15,000, or 20,000 years ago, but he had to keep his students busy doing something of local interest if he was going to rebuild his funding base to return to Africa.

The project under Russell required comparing three Paleoindian skulls from Alaska with a skull recently discovered by Russian archeologists in northeastern Siberia. All four skulls had been dated close to 10,000 years. The goal was to gain new insights on the Asian

31

origins of early Americans by looking for similarities between the skulls. The Alaskan skulls were matrix free, whereas, the Russian skulls, on loan from the Russian government, arrived in a block of hardened red sandstone. Fortunately, Russell was co-director of the Computed Tomography (CT) Laboratory and arranged for one of its staff to make a 3-D image of the Russian skull, which could then be translated into a wax copy using a 3-D printer. Slater could then mold and cast the copy for comparative purposes.

೫೫೫

Slater eventually made friends with some of the graduate students and established a rapport with Craig Russell, who was a member of his graduate committee. Russell looked every part the field anthropologist with his wiry frame, long hair, and mustache, all befitting his blue jeans, turquoise belt buckle, and worn Tony Lama boots, one of which had been repaired with duct tape. He was liked by his students for always taking time to answer questions, or letting students walk in and out of his office to borrow books or reprints from his extensive library, as long as they left a sign-out note in the shoebox by the door. Wilde, on the other hand, with the exception of his bushy, curly hair, looked like a walking Brooks Brothers catalog and communicated with students almost exclusively during office hours.

Slater usually spent his mornings at the main campus and his afternoons at the VP Lab. Sometimes he stopped for lunch at O's Cafe, the upscale cafeteria on the ground floor of the new Engineering Science Building, before heading to the north campus by bus or in his pickup.

On this early November day, a cool breeze blew through the open glass doors that led to an open courtyard. Slater ate alone, while skimming through the *Daily Texan*, the student newspaper. He caught a glimpse of two faculty members of the Anthropology Department walking by carrying trays. They sat at a table next to his, but a row of large leafy plants made Slater all but invisible. He thought they were cultural anthropologists specializing in Mexico prehistory.

He tried to ignore their gossipy conversation. They were clearly put out by one of their colleagues. Then the name Wilde came up.

"There is something decidedly fishy about this guy," one of them said. "He's received hundreds of thousands of dollars from NSF, but from what I understand not one cent of that money has followed him here from Harvard. Why in the hell else would he be hustling our money from the UT general science fund? It makes no sense."

Slater put down his newspaper.

"I agree," said the other, "it makes no sense whatsoever. Now the dean tells me I'll probably have to cancel my plans for Oaxaca this fall for lack of funds, which have been earmarked for over a year. Something stinks!"

"No kidding. And have you heard the latest dirt coming out of Harvard that was floating around the American Anthro meetings last week? Apparently, while in Cambridge, Wilde was a first-class womanizer, which included students."

"Yeah, I've heard that one. That was going on when he was at Rice as well, or so I've been told, even after he married one of his students who apparently inherited a swimming pool full of Exxon stock."

"But listen to this." The voice dropped in volume, but Slater could still hear him. "Now there's a rumor from Harvard that he actually raped one of his Ph.D. candidates, a 26-year-old, who then died of complications from an abortion."

Slater froze, staring at the wall.

"You're joking!"

"No shit. I've heard the same story from two sources and that snake reporter from *Science Report* was even asking about it."

. . . raped one of his students, who died from an abortion? Slater gasped.

"I tell you, this man is dangerous. And what's happened to his great African site all of a sudden? Not a word about it."

Slater could barely breathe. Surely "the student" they talked about couldn't have been Laura! But as conversations and events flashed through his mind from six months back, it suddenly all made sense. Could it be that Laura had the abortion not because it was his child, but because . . . If that's true, why didn't she confide in him? Slater jumped from his chair and raced out of the building.

Chapter 6

Cynthia's Story

Slater caught the first available flight to Boston he could get, charging it to his Visa card, then caught a taxi into Cambridge. In his haste, he gave the driver the wrong street number and had to walk some distance. The night was dark, overcast, and misty, with a chill in the air that helped clear his mind and sort out his questions. He could barely make out the street numbers. At last he found the right address. Cynthia had shared the second floor apartment with Laura for nearly two years in one of those rundown, partitioned mansions that grace the neighborhoods surrounding the Harvard campus.

At 11:15 he pushed the buzzer for the apartment of Cynthia Patterson, Laura's best friend and roommate. Slater tracked her down that afternoon on her cell phone. When she heard the tremor and urgency in his voice, she immediately knew the reason for his call. She was expecting him.

She buzzed back and heard his hurried footsteps on the stairs. Cynthia and Laura had been compatible roommates, keeping similar hours, liking the same kinds of music, and respecting one another's privacy. Both had been on-again, off-again vegetarians, and both drank too much coffee. Cynthia was an avid jogger. Laura took aerobics classes.

Slater wasted no time raising the reason for his late night visit. "Do you know anything about Laura being raped? Is this why she had an abortion?"

Cynthia lowered her head but said nothing.

Slater repeated the question. "Do you know anything about Laura being raped?"

Cynthia nodded, sobbing.

"Was it Wilde?"

"Yes, *yes* . . . that's what she told me!"

Slater, sitting in a worn-out easy chair, felt a shock ripple through his body. He felt nauseous, folded his arms across his stomach and leaned over, taking deep breaths through his teeth.

"Laura told me, but not before . . . " Cynthia struggled to regain her composure, "I left for Southeast Asia at the end of March to start . . . to start my botanical research. About a week after I arrived in Jarkata I received several long emails from her telling me the whole story . . . but, but I must . . . " Cynthia paused.

"Go on," said Slater, raising his head.

"But I have to tell you at the outset that I cannot prove what she told me because my laptop was stolen a week later."

"That's all right, I believe you."

And Laura had no doubt erased her emails before she died. Slater knew about that. She had a thing about saving "computer clutter."

Cynthia reconstructed the story as best as she could remember.

"In early April in the late afternoon, Wilde's secretary, Bette, a small Taiwanese woman, ran into Laura in the hallway of the Anthropology Department. Bette asked her if she'd mind dropping some papers off at Wilde's home, since she knew that Laura lived in that direction. 'Professor home all day, but he not sick I believe,' Bette explained, 'most unusual.' She seemed nervous and anxious to leave, except that she apparently had been instructed by higher-ups to hand over some papers to Wilde that day without fail. '*Very important,*' Bette emphasized.

"Laura readily agreed to do the errand and followed Bette back to her office to pick up the papers. They were contained in a large, sealed envelope, which Laura put in her book bag. As she started for the door, Bette called after her saying that she 'would call professor and tell him you on the way.' "

Slater recalled several visits to Wilde's home for gatherings and knew it well. It was a large, two-story, red brick home built in the mid-1800s, set back from the street by a well-kept lawn. The house contained two fireplaces downstairs and two upstairs, and was richly furnished with thick carpets, antiques, and bookcases filled with expensive, rare books. His last visit there with Laura in March was memorable. The occasion was to introduce the graduate students to a new faculty member, a specialist in Paleolithic European archeology. Ample wine and beer were served. Looking back, Slater recalled that Wilde spent some time talking with Laura, putting the charm on her, for which he was famous with the girls. They had laughed about it afterwards. But Laura felt flattered that he was interested in her work. Slater also recalled that Mrs. Wilde—an attractive woman he guessed in her mid-30s, but somewhat worn looking—got drunk and went around the living room insisting that everyone call her by her first name, Alice. She then led those interested—most of the students—on a tour of the house, every room, even the closets, saying over and over again that she and Bertie "had nothing to hide." The party broke up early.

Cynthia went on to explain that, "Laura went by Wilde's home, as requested. She rang the doorbell and removed the large envelope from her book bag. As she did, she couldn't help notice that the return address was Harvard's general counsel's office. Just at that moment the door opened and Wilde appeared. They exchanged greetings, but he looked angry, like he caught her looking into his private life. He snatched the envelope from Laura's hands, thanked her, and turned to close the door, but after a momentary pause turned back around and apologized for his abruptness. He then invited her in saying that his day had been extremely hectic, and that he had some very important information *about you*," Cynthia emphasized. She looked up at Slater. "He said he knew you and Laura were 'an item, or something to that effect.

"Concerned, Laura stepped inside and stood by the door. Wilde casually flipped the door lock before ushering her into the living room. He tossed the envelope on a chair, as if he already knew its contents, and allowed that his 'ditsy wife' was out of town. Laura suddenly felt decidedly uncomfortable, but Wilde became very cordial and gentlemanly. He invited her to sit by the lighted fireplace, which she did in a chair opposite his."

Slater tried to take in what he had just been told.

Cynthia paused, "You've heard that Wilde was fired by Harvard, right?"

"No, I didn't . . ." Slater said, "but I guess I've always suspected there was more to his move to Texas than was apparent."

"Well, there was. Some of the profs even talked about it to students, discreetly. Word is that it concerned how he got his grant money from NSF. I don't know the details, but it sounds pretty crooked—bribes, kickbacks, or something to that effect. This is only a guess, but the envelope that Laura delivered that day from Harvard's legal office probably had something to do with that, because Wilde left Harvard a few days later."

"Yes, that would have been in mid-April," Slater recalled.

Cynthia continued.

"Wilde told Laura that he had some bad news. Because of major funding cuts from his NSF grant, which supported your dissertation research, he could not see how you could remain at Harvard past the end of the semester, unless you came up with independent funding.

"Wilde said he wanted Laura to know this because he was aware how close you and she were, since you had slept together on his expeditions. Besides the substance of what he said, the tone of his voice frightened Laura. She became very upset and started to rise from her chair, but Wilde became very apologetic and offered her a small glass of wine to calm her nerves, which she accepted and drank right away. Within a few minutes, however, she became woozy and disoriented, as if the wine were drugged. Realizing that it might have been, she again rose to leave, but Wilde's large frame blocked her way. He then awkwardly hugged her in a fatherly way. The hug, however, didn't stop there; Wilde began groping her. Laura had no strength to fight him or even to scream. She felt like she was going to blackout, which she did. The next thing she realized she was on the carpeted floor with Wilde on top of her. She tried again to scream, but Wilde put his hand over her mouth and told her to 'Shut the hell up.'

"When he was finished, she realized she was totally nude. As she gathered her clothes and got dressed, Wilde stood by without saying a word. She had no idea how long she had been unconscious, except that it was dark outside. When she stood up she could feel semen, or blood, or both, running down her legs.

"Finally, Wilde said he didn't know what came over him, he was desperately sorry, and that he must have had some kind of a nervous breakdown—he had been under tremendous pressure lately. He told her he was sure he could find a way to keep you at Harvard after all, as long as she kept this 'little incident' between them. If he heard one peep about this 'your boyfriend will be history; in fact, he could become prehistory.' Laura stumbled out the door and ran down the steps. 'Remember what I told you!' Wilde called out to her."

As Cynthia talked, Slater sat quietly; his hands shook as he alternately stared at the floor or at a small framed photograph on the wall of Laura and Cynthia. They stood in the snow with their coats and mittens on, laughing. Both were covered with splotches of snow and their cheeks were red. As he looked at the photo, Slater felt as if his insides were boiling and the story he had just heard was shouted at him from the end of a tunnel, with the words echoing and reverberating through his brain. How could this possibly have happened to Laura without his knowledge? He was dumbfounded that he hadn't sensed the upheaval that had torn through her life.

"The next thing I heard," Cynthia continued, "after spending four months in the rain forest, was on my return to the U.S. in mid-July. I was devastated to learn that Laura had died during an abortion. I could not believe it! I couldn't believe that she died, and I couldn't believe that you went to Texas with that monster. Frankly, that made me suspicious of you, like you had struck some kind of deal with the devil."

"I understand," Slater said. "I had made a deal with the devil—I just didn't know it. By bringing me to Texas, Wilde was able to keep me out of Cambridge, where I might have somehow put this together before now and done something about it."

"I'm sorry I didn't reach you," Cynthia said earnestly. "Stories are still going around about Wilde. Finally, I concluded that Laura simply had not told you before she died. She was so mortified. I tried to call you in Austin when I returned, but was told you were off in West Texas or somewhere. Then from September until just last week I was traveling visiting museum collections."

After Cynthia put on a pot of coffee, she and Slater

spent the next two hours talking—going over and over again what they both knew of Wilde, especially his relationships with female students. At least now Slater knew why Laura had kept the matter from him. Wilde had warned her to keep quiet, or he would be gone. And what else did he say, that he, Slater, "could become prehistory"? What kind of threat was this? Had Laura told him, he would have gone immediately to the police and to the university authorities. Maybe Laura was afraid of that too. Perhaps she was afraid that her fundamentalist parents would insist she keep the baby.

They talked more about why Wilde left Harvard. They wondered whether there was any connection with Laura's rape, but ruled that out because surely Harvard would have gone straight to the police. On the other hand, it would have caused a monumental scandal for the university and there is no telling what tact Wilde might have taken.

The issue was what to do next. Wilde was still powerful and obviously a vicious man. Exhausted, Slater took a taxi back to Logan Airport, arriving at 3:00 a.m. He slept on the floor near the Delta gate until it was time to board his 6:00 flight back to Texas.

Chapter 7

Presidio County

As Thanksgiving neared, Wilde felt the heat building daily. He knew, rather sensed, the rumors were making their way from Cambridge to Austin. He was desperate to retain his proper place in the pantheon of science. Returning to Africa was out, at least for now, until he could land some big donors. He figured he'd need twice the money he had before to overcome the opposition. He even read the obituaries looking for a middle-aged widow left with acreage in downtown Dallas who might take a shine to anthropology.

And then there were the patrons of his father's church, but since Bert had long ago rejected the spiritual world for the earthly world, he wasn't about to feign religion at this stage in his life. True, he had access to Alice's finances, but pouring "his" own assets into Africa to win back concessions was out of the question. No, he wouldn't go that route.

What about Texas? He had grown sick of hearing about Clovis projectile points. And the "Leanderthal woman" for Christ's sake, a 10,000-year-old female skeleton found in the town of Leander near Austin in the early 1980s, which by all accounts raised hysteria with the creationists. Hell, in Africa, humans that old still lived.

In the 1950s the fossil skull of a lemur-like prosimian was found in the Big Bend, but it was among the most primitive of primates, one that lived off leaves, hardly on the lineage of humankind. No, Wilde had to find something big and glossy to keep his reputation and the influence he once wielded, especially with the eager female graduate students who couldn't resist his animal magnetism, and the academic favors that came with it.

As for Alice, she was fully aware that she was locked into a marriage with a man she increasingly feared. During his last month at Harvard, when things were obviously going terribly wrong, he repeatedly had violent bursts of temper, saying how he would like to kill this person or that. She welcomed the move to Austin, hoping the change would offer new opportunities for her husband, and perhaps for their marriage. She had never felt part of the Cambridge community, which she considered elitist and cold. She loved their new home in Austin, located one mile west of the university in exclusive Pemberton Heights, a large Spanish style house with a courtyard and a red tiled roof, set among large pecan and oak trees. She was still determined to have children, but she was also aware that at age thirty-five time was running out.

৩৩৩৩

On his return to Austin from Cambridge, Slater became ill and didn't stir from his apartment, ignoring telephone calls and the occasional knock on his door.

Periodically, he ate whatever food he could, but couldn't hold it down.

Sleep dissolved into visions of a bloodied Laura with a menacing Wilde standing over her. He'd awake in a pool of sweat like he was afflicted with an exotic African fever. Finally, after five days, he roused himself, drawing on whatever restorative powers he had; he knew that Laura would expect him to go forward.

Explaining his week-long absence, weight loss, and pallid look, Slater told people he had suffered from food poisoning. As the Christmas holidays approached, he regained his strength and worked harder than ever. Over the next month, he resumed his routine of working in the Anthropology Department in the mornings and at the VP Lab at the north campus in the afternoons. He sometimes worked at the lab into the night, obtaining a special permit from the campus police to be there after hours.

He could also be seen going in and out of the Anthropology Department well before classes began to complete his project for Russell comparing the Alaskan Paleoindian and Russian skulls. The CT scans of the latter, imbedded in sandstone, and the 3-D casts he made from a wax copy, revealed strong similarities between the two samples, suggesting similar Siberian origins.

A more detailed analysis of the fossils was beyond the scope of Slater's study. At this stage, it was enough to demonstrate to the Russian archeologists the non-invasive nature of the CT technology and to urge further collaboration on human origins between researchers in eastern Asia and North America.

In his research paper for Wilde on faunal migrations,

Slater provided detailed accounts of the known movements of the woolly mammoth, musk ox, bear, moose, wolf, and other cold-adapted animals into North America during the Pleistocene glacial periods. He also provided some intriguing new data from the Bering Sea. Cores from off-shore wells indicated that tectonic uplift in the early Pleistocene, apparently caused by shifting plates, created a temporary land bridge across Beringia during a temperate period, allowing animals adapted to warmer temperatures to cross into the New World.

Finally, Slater completed provisional descriptions and identities of the Scorpion Arroyo fossils and submitted his findings to Wilde, which included a description of the geology of the site, and detailed maps showing the location by catalog number of each specimen collected in the test pits he had excavated. He also removed the sandstone matrix from key fossils and reconstructed broken specimens.

Wilde later flipped through the two reports in his office and read the summaries of each. He scanned Slater's field report first.

Presidio County, the "Sahara of Texas," he thought, as he tossed the report down and picked up the faunal migrations report. He did not give a damn about the travels of "woolly animals" in the northern latitudes, or their warmth-loving relatives to the south, but there was some interesting data about tectonic uplift in Beringia.

"Wait a minute, Presidio County!"

Chapter 8

Pig Man

With the holidays just beginning, the newly appointed Director of the UT Visitor's Center called the Director of Public Relations to say, "I have two gentlemen here waiting to see me. Right now they are looking at our displays, that is, they're hitting up my secretary."

"Pretty good looking is she?"

"She's engaged."

"Pretty good looking?"

"An abundance."

"An abundance of what?"

"Everything."

"Maybe we should all have lunch sometime. What's on your mind?"

"As I was saying, these men are asking to see some 'petrified animals' collected by UT researchers on their ranch in Presidio County. Mammoths, that sort of thing. They sound a bit funky so I thought I would check with you."

"So, you think I'm in charge of weirdoes?"

"No, no, but as I recall you are from that part of the state, near the Mexican border, right?"

"Where'd you say you're from again, *amigo*, Iowa?"

"Delaware."

"Delaware? Where in the *hell* is Delaware?"

"It's on the East Coast near …"

"That's okay. I'm from Amarillo. That's about 5,000 miles from the Mexican border. You better learn some Texas geography. What are the names of these men?"

"They're both named Harrington. They must be brothers. Heard of them?"

"Nope, never heard of them."

"They say they're long-time supporters of UT research, although I've checked our database of donors and we've got nothing on them. They strike me as West Texas oilmen types, or cattlemen."

"How'ze that? They got West Texas crude or shit on their boots?"

"Uh . . . "

"Tell you what, forget the database. It sounds like they're asking about mammalian fossils and that would be the province of the Vertebrate Paleontology Laboratory, which is administered by the Texas Memorial Museum. It so happens I'm on the museum's board of directors and I know the VP Lab is in serious need of expansion. More work space for students and visitors, and more fossils. Maybe we can spring some bucks from these guys. Let me give Bert Wilde in the Anthropology Department a call and I'll get back to you. He's connected to the lab and a new faculty guru. Mainly, he's a real hustler for funds."

"That would be great."

"And don't forget that lunch. *Adíos*."

The PR officer then contacted Wilde, who he knew

from museum functions, to see if he could show the men around the VP Lab. Wilde, himself sensing a new funding opportunity, immediately agreed to give them a tour. He called Slater and asked him if he would help escort the visitors around the lab and show them the fossils he had collected on their ranch. Slater agreed. More importantly, Wilde hoped the visit would give him the opportunity to talk to the men about bankrolling an expedition in Africa.

By arrangement, the next afternoon the two visitors were driven in a UT van from the main campus to the lab to meet Wilde and Slater. Slater arrived a few minutes early. The technicians, research staff, and students, normally bustling throughout the building, had long since left to beat the holiday traffic. Scattered around the lab were paper cups, some partially filled with punch, and paper plates containing crumbs or bits of homemade cookies. The remains of the annual holiday party held after lunch. Slater quickly cleared away the trash just before the van arrived with the visitors, whom he warmly welcomed.

Wilde arrived ten minutes later and quickly pegged one of the men as a "fossil freak," who said he had found a "cement horse" and a "rock mammodont" on his ranch.

The other claimed he had found "butt loads of arrowheads on the ranch," which he "glued above every doorway in his house."

"You ought to see those suckers," he told Wilde enthusiastically. "When I was a kid I found 'em all over the ranch. Makes you wonder how many white folks those arrowheads split open, don't it?"

Not enough, Wilde thought to himself. "I'm sure quite a few, Mr. . . . ah?"

"Harrington," said Roper.

"Right. Harrington," replied Rider.

"So, you two are . . . related?"

"It's worse than that, we're twins," Roper answered.

"I should have guessed."

They were not exactly identical, however, since a lifetime of ranching had left Roper's face and the back of his hands deeply tanned and wrinkled. A white band across his forehead resulted from his cowboy hat, which he seldom removed. Rider was pale by comparison, since he spent most days running the family hardware store in Marfa. Both were married with grown children, and the same in-laws, since they had married sisters, Edora and Eudora. They were a close family.

As Wilde wondered how best to shorten the tour, Slater was already showing the men around the preparation room. The tools and materials used by the lab technicians and students were scattered about at workstations.

He pointed to some fossils propped up on sandbags and in sandboxes in various stages of reconstruction. "Over here on this table we have a triceratops skull from Big Bend National Park that's approximately 100 million years old."

"Wow," said Rider, slapping Roper on the back as if he were trying to kill a horsefly. "That's almost as old as your wife, *har, har, har!*"

"Hey," said Roper, "that hurt!"

"And over here next to the window," Slater continued, "we have the lower jaw of a giant crocodile from the Coal Mine Ranch. It's approximately the same age as the triceratops skull. The complete animal was probably close to 30 feet in length and weighed up to seven tons."

"*Whoa*, that's it," said Roper. "No more swimming in the Rio Grande for me. I wonder how many politicians one of those meat factories could eat in one day?"

As they moved on, Rider picked up a skull. "What's this guy, a coyote?"

"It's called a *Hyaenodon*. You're right, it's a carnivore," replied Slater. "This animal lived between 36 and 38 million years ago."

"How can you know its age that closely, voodoo?" asked Roper.

"Not voodoo. This specimen has been dated radiometrically, in a manner similar to carbon-14 dating. The age is based on the rate of decay of naturally occurring radioactive minerals present in volcanic rocks. West Texas is full of strata of volcanic origin that allow us to date fossils very closely."

"What's this ugly creature, a saber-toothed cocker spaniel?" asked Roper.

"Close enough. It's a saber-toothed cat from a cave near San Antonio."

"How old is . . . ?"

Impatient with all the nonsense, Wilde looked at his watch and said, "I am afraid we're going to have to quickly move on. Lots of holiday traffic today."

Next came the always popular "bug room" at the far end of the collections area. There, in a large, screened-in cage, dermestid beetles were busy enjoying the final remains of a bighorn sheep. Momentarily ignoring complaints from the twins of the "gawd awful stench," Slater explained that dead animals were donated to the lab by zoos and road-kill enthusiasts around the state. The carcasses were defleshed by hungry bugs, then soaked and scrubbed with diluted ammonia until they were free of all blood and flesh. Students or researchers can then use the bleached bones for comparative purposes when studying their fossil counterparts.

"These bones look like some of our Christmas dinners on the ranch, before the meal was served!" Rider volunteered.

After a tour of the vertebrate fossils stored in fireproof cabinets on the main floor and a trip to the basement to see dinosaur fossils stored on shelves, Wilde told the brothers he had a special treat for them as he led the way into the lecture room. "Mr. Slater, one of my doctoral students, will now show you a major discovery he made from right down there in your very own Presidio County." The Scorpion Arroyo collection was laid out on two long tables placed end to end.

Roper looked at Rider and raised his eyebrows, as if to say, "No kidding!"

"These fossils are one *million* years old!" Wilde boasted.

"Actually, I'm guessing their age is closer to 1.5 million years old," Slater interjected. "We have no radiometric dates to confirm this, but the assemblage of fossils is similar enough to those dated elsewhere to support the older age."

"Even better!" said Wilde. "Certainly this trove of fossils from your county is one of the greatest scientific discoveries made in Texas."

"Hold on! Just hold it right there, professor," said

Roper, while looking at Ron. "My brother and I know exactly where these fossils come from in Presidio County, but do you know?"

"Well, I just assumed that Ron . . ."

"They come from the Double-H Ranch, which my brother and I own. The land was originally purchased by our family in 1881 and we've knowd there are fossils there ever since. That's because when Captain Jacob Harrington, our great-granddaddy, completed the big house, he cemented a mammodon tusk between stones above the fire place and it's still there!"

"Fascinating. I'm truly embarrassed not to have known this history," said Wilde. "Is all this contained in your report, Ron?" he asked sternly.

"No, I . . ."

"I'm sure it's not," said Roper. "I'd forgotten all about that tusk, which I guess could've come from anywhere on the ranch."

"Just about," Ron agreed.

"How about the Captain's exploits during the Civil War," Rider asked Wilde, "do you know about that?"

"No, but some other time. Ron, why don't you show these gentleman what fossils you have here?" Wilde asked. *Then we can get these yahoos out the door*, he thought.

Slater looked at Roper, who nodded his head, "Let's see what ya got." For the next fifteen minutes Slater picked up fossils one by one while handing them to their guests. As he did so, he gave a brief commentary of each.

"This is a molar of a mammoth, an animal closely related to living Asian elephants, often confused with mastodons, which is actually a much more primitive creature. You can see the mammoth tooth is roughly shaped like a loaf of bread. In contrast the surface of unworn mastodon teeth is shaped like rows of female breasts, which is how mastodons got their name. *Mast* in Greek means breast; *dont* means tooth."

Roper and Rider were listening with rapt attention. "Rows of breasts," said Rider. "This is starting to get really interesting."

Next, Slater picked up a tooth that looked like a giant cow molar. "This tooth belonged to a giant bison, a large herbivore with horns up to ten feet across. This animal is closely related to living buffalo, but became extinct in North America about 10,000 years ago, along with mammoths, horses, camels, and a number of other animals. Some scholars believe the extinction of these large animals was due to Indian hunters; others attribute the extinctions to climate changes."

"Wait a minute, horses are still around," said Roper and Rider simultaneously.

"Yes and no. Horses first appear in the fossil record of North America about 35 million years ago and disappeared at the end of the Ice Age about 10,000 years ago. But then they were reintroduced by the Spaniards about 9,500 years after that.

"We all know what happened next," said Roper. "The Comanches and the Apaches got ahold of those Spanish horses, and rifles, and that's when it hit the fan. But you mentioned camels. You're not saying they originated here too?"

"Yep, camels originated in North America about the same time as horses."

"Now you're going off the deep end," protested Roper. "Everyone in this part of the country knows that Jefferson Davis brought 'em here to carry mail across the desert, and that wasn't no millions of years ago."

"Well, there's much to learn," interrupted Wilde, "and it's time we move on."

"You bet there's much to learn," interrupted Rider. "You ain't seen nothing 'til you've seen the killer jackrabbits living in caves up in the mountains on our ranch. With my own eyes, I seen 'em run down from the hills and rip the tires off a tractor, and that's no shit! If anyone is stupid enough to hunt 'em, they damn sure better have a high-powered rifle or a 12-gauge shotgun with slugs in it, 'cause if they charge . . . ."

"Excuse me!" said Wilde looking at his watch, "we had better wrap this up, otherwise the traffic . . .will . . ." As Slater made his presentation, Wilde continued to pace around the room looking bored, while occasionally reaching down to pick up a fossil. He stopped for a moment at the far end of the table and picked up a partial jaw bearing the remains of a few flat, square teeth.

"Mother of Jesus!" he muttered under his breath. He was speechless. He felt his heart pound. His hands trembled as he held the jaw fragment. What the hell? "And what do we have here Ron?" he said, regaining his composure.

"Although it's only a fragment, I'm guessing it's a partial upper jaw of a large tayassuid."

"Tanya Sue who?" Rider asked. "Sounds like someone I used to date in high school. Cheerleader at that."

Although clearly distracted, Wilde interjected, "Pig. That's short for pig. I mean it's a pig. Ron is saying the fossil belongs to the zoological family Tayassuidae. Very good, Ron, I agree. Pig for sure."

"But then again," Roper offered, "it could be a chicken dressed like a pig, right? Ride on?"

"Could be."

"The kind of animal we're talking about is a peccary, although most people know them as *javelinas*," Slater explained.

"Don't I know it," Roper said. "The tusks on one of those big males can rip open a hound dog like a can of sardines."

Pig, peccary, javelina, my ass! Wilde said to himself, as he casually put the specimen back down on the tray and let Slater describe the rest of the collection.

"Now this one is interesting," said Slater. "These are the teeth of a small horse about the size of . . ."

In the twelve seconds that Wilde got a good look at the fossil he came to his own conclusions: *That's a goddamn maxilla fragment of an early Homo if I ever saw one. The third molar and some of the surrounding bone on the left side were missing, but portions of the second and first molars were present, as was the second premolar. The molars were badly worn and crushed, but the overall shape and configuration of what remained of the dentition, the sockets of the missing teeth, and the palate margin revealed a distinct outward bowing of the tooth row. If the maxilla was complete, he was certain the alignment of the dentition would be parabolic in shape, a defining feature of the genus Homo.*

How old did Slater estimate these fossils were, 1.5 million years? In North America? That's impossible! And what was it that Slater had written in his research paper, something about the uplift of Beringia may have formed a land bridge during a warm period in the early Pleistocene?

Wilde was furiously trying to focus his thoughts. He had to get these buffoons out of here and look at that fossil again.

"Well, professor, it's been a very interesting tour," Rider said, bringing Wilde back from the Pleistocene. "Thank you kindly."

"Yes, very educational, surely," said Roper. "Now we know what you do with these fossils, more or less. Ron, come visit us again soon. Bring the professor with you, if he's not too scared of snakes and goon bugs. Hell, we'll even teach him how to ride a mule deer."

"What are 'goon bugs'?" Wilde asked with his mind still distant.

"Goon bugs? You ain't never heard of goon bugs?" asked Rider. "Goon bugs is chiggers. You get enough chigger bites and you go goony, *har, har, har*."

Wilde hadn't even approached the two about backing an expedition to Africa. All he could say was, "Thank you both for dropping by, Mr. . . . Harrison?"

"Wrong!" corrected Rider. "It's Har-ring-ton."

"Very sorry," said Wilde, "and yours is the Double-H Ranch, correct?" recalling more details from Slater's report.

"That's the one," said Roper.

"And you're both in the oil business?" Wilde asked.

"The what? You gotta be kidding!" said Rider. "The only oil I've seen comes out of the bottom of Roper's pickup."

Son of a bitch, Wilde thought, and I wasted my time on these dimwits.

"Ron, why don't you take these men back to their hotel—*or to their cave*—in the department van. Just park it next to the Anthropology Building and leave the keys in the drop box. I'll lock up the lab."

"Sure," Slater replied.

They all walked outside to the parking lot where Wilde shook hands with the two men. The van from the Visitor's Center was waiting for them.

He wished the three of them a Merry Christmas. As they drove off, Wilde looked at his watch and hurried back inside. It was 4:30.

Chapter 9

Slater's Report

Wilde hurried through the building making sure no one remained and that all the doors were locked. He immediately returned to the classroom, picked up the jaw fragment, and took it over to a table containing a binocular microscope. He sat down, flipped on its light, and examined the specimen again, very closely.

Next, he grabbed a needle vise off a table in the workroom and made a tiny scratch on the inside surface of the bone and examined it under the microscope at high power, then medium power, low power, and back and forth again.

"*Bone beneath bone*. Son of a bitch, this is the genuine article," he whispered. He felt certain that the low-crowned, square shape of what remained of the molars, and the curvature of the molar row, was classic *Homo*. He hadn't studied hominid dentition for 20 years for nothing! To the untrained eye, he could conceive how the broken and deeply worn molars could be mistaken for tayassuid teeth. Certainly, Slater was not the first graduate student to mistake human teeth for pigs, or vice versa.

After all, the renowned Henry Fairfield Osborn,

president of the American Museum of Natural History, made one of the most famous misidentifications in paleoanthropology when he confused a pig tooth with an ape molar. In 1922, he blitzed the scientific literature with a series of papers describing a single, worn tayassuid molar from Nebraska as an anthropoid primate, which he named *Hesperopithecus*—"Ape of the Western World."

Unfortunately, five years later "Nebraska Man" was correctly identified as "Pig Man," much to the glee of Osborn's detractors, among them the vociferous opponent of Darwinism, William Jennings Bryan, who happened to be from Nebraska.

Before going off the deep end, Wilde was well aware that his putative hominid fossil was still only a partial jaw, and its identity required unequivocal confirmation. He knew he would have to extract every square micron of information from the specimen before going public. His critics would become hysterical in any case. A human fossil 1.5 million years old, some 50,000 generations older than the oldest known human remains in North America? They would laugh him off the continent, at least initially.

He turned off the microscope light, walked into the next room to a storage cabinet, and removed a small specimen box. He used cotton to carefully pack the fossil inside the box, which he wrapped with rubber bands and placed snugly in a zippered inside breast pocket of his jacket. He then used the wall phone to see if by any chance Craig Russell was still in his office. No answer. He would catch him later.

Wilde knew Russell planned to stay in town during the holidays. He hoped Russell could get one of his colleagues in the CT Lab to scan the fossil the first thing the next day for a look at its internal morphology.

Now what had Slater written in his report about Beringia?

On his way home Wilde stopped by his office and picked up Slater's Presidio field report and research paper. He retrieved both from a neat pile of other student papers on a shelf in his meticulously kept office. Wilde believed that an organized work place reflected an organized mind. Everything, like every person, had its place. That's why he refused to allow his wife to cross the threshold of his study at their home.

 C8C8C8

At dinner, with his mind completely preoccupied, Alice talked about her day. "You'll be interested to know that I've joined a health club. In addition, I've signed up for an advanced course in watercolors at the university, since everyone thinks I'm *sooo* talented. The instructor is wonderful. He's about my age and . . ."

Wilde finished the last bite on his plate and immediately arose from his chair and headed for his study. During the meal he had said nothing nor listened to a word Alice said, but as he left the table he noticed that she had not touched her glass of wine. Unusual.

When Alice heard the door to his study close, she continued, " . . . he's very good looking. We had coffee together, then lunch, and then we went to his studio. We will meet again soon. It's amazing, but we just click. It so happens he's single and he loves children. We get along very well. And between you and me, Bertie, I think he finds me intelligent as well as attractive. Isn't that nice?"

Wilde's study was filled with the same rare and expensive books that filled the shelves of his Cambridge home, except that now his walls were hung with early maps of Texas, instead of those of Massachusetts. He pulled Slater's two reports from his briefcase and set them down beside his favorite chair, facing the fireplace. He switched on his reading lamp. Since the night was cold, he turned on the gas jets beneath the oak logs, lighted them with a fire starter until flames appeared, and then turned off the gas.

One comfort he shared with Alice: they both liked to keep the house cool enough in the winter to keep a fire going, Austin's mild winters permitting. Their house, built at the turn of the century, featured fireplaces in the living room, the master bedroom, and in his study.

As he stood watching the fire sweep from one log to the next, a thought crossed his mind. What if someone turned on the gas in their bedroom fireplace without remembering to light the fire, say Alice, when she was dead drunk? He wondered how long it would take for her to become asphyxiated, assuming the windows and doors were tightly shut? Since they both used his attorney, he knew for a fact that she had not drawn up a will of her own, nor did he encourage her to. According to Texas law, if she were to die without a will, with no children or siblings, the bereaved husband would inherit everything.

Before turning to Slater's reports, Wilde walked across the room, used the combination lock to open his private liquor cabinet, and pulled out a bottle of fine brandy. After pouring himself a small glass, he replaced the bottle and relocked the cabinet. Finally, he sat down to read Slater's first report on faunal migrations from Asia to North America.

The report was 61 pages long with 23 pages of references and notes. He had to hand it to the kid, he was thorough, even though he had misidentified the greatest find of his career. He had to feel sorry for him, losing his girlfriend and all that. God, what a screw-up that had been!

Wilde took a sip of brandy, then from a side table pulled out a dark leaf Dominican cigar. He lit it, drawing in the rich Caribbean tobacco, while opening Slater's report. It highlighted the latest data on Pleistocene sea level changes, giving maximum lows accompanying colder temperatures, and times when cold-adapted animals could have crossed Beringia. In his discussion, however, he devoted only two brief paragraphs to what was surely the most significant part of the paper.

Between about 1.6 and 1.4 million years ago, there had been a brief but intense period of tectonic activity in the Bering Strait, apparently related to plate movement in the northern Pacific. This event happened to coincide with a warming trend, when a rise in global sea levels due to ice melt would normally submerge much of Beringia. As revealed by fossil pollen recovered from cores obtained by offshore drilling, however, tectonic uplift nevertheless created a land bridge estimated at 75 to 110 miles wide and 90 miles across, connecting the Siberian and Alaskan mainlands. The pollen indicated a steppe-like environment with freshwater lakes apparently covering much of the exposed land area. After approximately 45,000 years, renewed tectonism caused the land bridge to subside beneath the sea.

Slater's sources mentioned nothing about paleofauna, although he noted that such a land bridge, as ephemeral as it was, could have easily allowed animals adapted to temperate conditions to migrate from Asia into North America and vice versa. Slater didn't mention possible human migrations. He didn't need to. Everything implied it. Wilde looked at Slater's references. He had documented the land bridge event from a dozen sources.

There it is! Wilde drew on his cigar, the blue-gray smoke trailing toward the fireplace. So for 45,000 years, the window of opportunity remained opened in the early Pleistocene, when early humans could have made their move into the New World without drowning or turning into ice art. These proto-Americans, probably small bands, made their way across Beringia, then headed south to warmer climates until at least one group reached the Rio Grande Valley. Their remains were preserved in alluvial rift sediments along with those of other Asian immigrants, such as mammoths, which early on had shed their shaggy coats.

Now Wilde had a working hypothesis to explain how early *Homo* could have reached North America. What happened to these early immigrants to cause their apparent extinction so quickly was another question. Disease? Climate change? Fratricide? He would deal with that later. He swirled the last of the brandy around his glass, and finished it off, then took a few more drags from his cigar and flipped the rest of it into the dwindling fire. Before leaving the room he made sure the gas was securely turned off and the windows were tightly closed.

Chapter 10

The Greatest

The next morning with the students gone for the holidays, Wilde enlisted Russell to arrange for the CT Lab to scan the jaw ahead of a backlog of other requests. As they walked over to the Geology Building where the lab was located, Russell asked Wilde what was so special about this particular jaw fragment, which he had shown him just minutes before.

"What's the big deal, Bert? This is hardly cover girl material for *Nature*."

"Just some leftover business from Africa, but please keep it to yourself. I agree it's no big deal."

Russell readily agreed it was hominid, but that was typical of Wilde's world. Everything was always urgent and vague, *hush hush*, or "I'll fill you in later," as if he were drawing up plans to invade Portugal.

In fact, Wilde wanted to compare the shape and configuration of the roots and tooth sockets of the Scorpion jaw with that of a modern human skull he brought with him from the Anthropology Department. After the jaws of both specimens were scanned, Wilde and Russell studied the results to confirm what they both expected. The two jaws were indeed similar, although the Scorpion jaw was more robust.

Wilde and Russell then walked over to the Anthropology Department and compared the Scorpion specimen to casts of *Homo* crania from Africa and Eurasia, particularly those of early Pleistocene age. Once again they concluded that the partial jaw was *Homo*, and once again Russell was puzzled why Wilde was so interested in this one scrappy specimen.

∽∾∽∾∽∾

The night before, Wilde had also read Slater's field report describing the geology and geography of the Scorpion Arroyo fossil site. Wilde had trained him well. The locality and specimen numbers of each fossil Slater recovered in his test pits were noted both in his field catalog of fossils and on the field maps he had carefully drawn of the site. The position of the "pig" jaw locality was noted in the northwest quadrant of test pit C. Wilde knew it was decidedly a long shot, but he pinned his hopes on finding more of the *Homo* skull near the spot where the jaw was located, particularly since a complete cranium of an antelope was found nearby, indicating the sometimes excellent preservation of fossils in the bone layer.

The next morning, December 18, Wilde left a message on Russell's voice mail telling him he was going to Bell County, 35 miles northeast of Austin, to meet with Ben Schultz, an aging rancher. His ranch was famous for containing the most prolific Clovis site known in North America. Wilde was scheming to get Schultz to deed the land in his will to a field school for Clovis studies, or to himself, in order to prepare students for archeological fieldwork in Africa.

ᏣᏣᏣ

Alice stood on the kitchen steps of their home in the morning chill watching Wilde load his Land Rover parked in the driveway. "Are you going to be gone long?"

"I shouldn't be, but don't worry, there's plenty of vodka in the whiskey closet."

Alice immediately returned to the house. Instead of reacting to the insult, as she normally would, she watched through the kitchen window as Wilde backed out of the drive and disappeared down the street. She picked up the wall telephone next to the sink and called Peter, her art instructor. "Guess what, I'm free for the next few days!"

ᏣᏣᏣ

Without looking back, Wilde drove through Pemberton Heights onto Windsor Road, then south on Loop One—the opposite direction from the Bell County Clovis site—and west on Highway 290. At Fredericksburg, he grabbed a pastry from a German bakery and continued west on 290. After hitting Interstate 10, he crossed the Trans-Pecos until he reached Fort Stockton where he stopped for lunch at Cattleman's Steak House. From there he drove southwest on Highway 67 through Alpine, Marfa, and Shafter, until he finally entered the Rio Grande Valley and the small desert town of Presidio in the late afternoon.

He had heard the area was in a severe drought, which

accounted for the barren and lifeless countryside. On the other hand, the sedimentary exposures were magnificent. He understood why Slater had chosen this area for his fieldwork.

Wilde checked into the better of the only two motels in Presidio, the Three Palms. He paid cash for a room, gave the clerk an extra $300 and told him he wanted something "warm, soft, and *supremo*" to knock on his door at eight o'clock sharp. "And if she gives me AIDS, I'll come back and kill you," he added.

The clerk took the money, forced a smile, and said, "Nothing but the best."

Wilde had dinner at the El Patio Café a few blocks away, then went back to his motel to shower and rest up for the evening's program.

ೞೞೞ

By ten the next morning he had already found the Scorpion Arroyo site using Slater's sketch map. He parked his Land Rover out of sight behind a bend on a gravel road passing through the Double-H Ranch, as Slater had done. He knew he wouldn't encounter the Harringtons because one had mentioned they planned to stay in Austin until just before Christmas.

Before long, Wilde found the four test pits and cleared away the brush thrown over them. It didn't take him long to find the spot where the "pig" jaw was recovered from test pit C. He was impressed by the preservation of fossils in sands beneath the gravels, as Slater had described in his report, and he agreed that the bones on the surface resulted from a flood event. Heavy rains had likely moved animal parts down an ancient stream channel and across a floodplain. He spent several hours excavating deeper into test pit C. He dug down: six inches, then twelve inches, then eighteen, but found nothing hominid. He did find more fossils, altogether a virtual Noah's Ark, as was apparent from Slater's collection back in the VP Lab. Now all he had to do was to find Noah.

By noon he was worn out and stopped for lunch. He wasn't used to such exercise. From his pack he grabbed two ham sandwiches filled with *jalapeños* that he picked up that morning at a convenience store, along with three large bottles of Gator Aid. He retrieved one bottle from an ice chest in the back of his Land Rover, and sat down with his back to a small knoll to break the cold wind. To the north, the Rio Grande flowed between mountains on either side of the river. He had to admit it was a beautiful setting, framed in a spotless blue sky. At seven that morning a flashing sign on the bank down the street from the motel had read 37 degrees. He guessed it was now close to 70 degrees. As he ate his lunch he thought about his visitor the previous evening. What a knockout! Well worth what he had spent on "field expenses."

σσσ

Wilde was discouraged. Finding more of the skull had seemed so "logical," but realistically, the project could take months of work involving a horde of excavators, with no guarantee of success. As he pondered this, he looked again at the spot where the hominid jaw was found in the northwest quadrant of test pit C. He realized he had not removed any of the gravel overlying the sand nearest the hominid locality; he had only excavated areas where Slater had already removed gravel. After finishing his lunch, he began expanding the pit to the northwest. His hands were already raw and blistered, since in his haste to leave Austin, he had forgotten to bring work gloves. Fortunately, most of the gravel was loose and easily removed.

After three hours of hard labor, he had cleared away another sixteen square feet of overburden and had begun excavating the underlying sand, but found fewer and fewer fossils. Then, after another 45 minutes he came upon a smooth rounded bone surface. A cranium?

Now don't jump to conclusions he told himself.

He grabbed a brush and methodically began clearing away the sand. Suddenly, something or someone caught his attention. In the direction of his vehicle, not more than a hundred feet away, a girl stood watching him. "Oh great, it's a goddamn wetback."

Wilde jumped up. "Border Patrol," he shouted. "Get the hell outta here!"

She continued to stand there.

He reached into his pack and pulled out a 38-caliber Smith & Wesson revolver. Pointing it at her, he yelled again, "Go! Go!"

That did the trick. She immediately started running away. He ran after her for 15 or 20 yards to show her he was serious, then stopped. He was breathing hard, too hard. He felt faint, but the girl dropped into another arroyo and disappeared.

He put his hands on his knees and struggled to catch

his breath. He lifted his head up and yelled, "Goddamn *puta*. Wetback! That's all I need is to shoot a Mexican," he said to himself. "With my luck, she's the daughter of a drug lord."

He returned to his excavation. He *had* found a rounded bone surface.

He brushed away more loose sand. He quickly looked around to make sure the girl was gone. No one in sight.

More sand.

His hands trembled.

More sand.

Slowly the features of a skull appeared. "Son of a bitch, it sure as hell looks like a human cranium." He took a deep breath. "Absolutely!"

He couldn't believe his eyes. Lying on its left side, he saw a jutting face and a sloping forehead. He dug further around the fossil, and slowly removed it with his hands. He looked again at the spot where he found the skull.

He had spent hours digging in all the wrong places when all the time the cranium was beneath the gravels only a few feet from where Slater had found the jaw fragment. He laid the skull on his knees, face up, continuing to brush and scrape away sand.

"Holy shit," he kept repeating. "Holy shit." He realized his hands were shaking, so he put the skull down, drew in a few deep breaths, then took an inventory of the skull's features: heavy brow ridges, prominent cheekbones, protruding lower face, and a surprisingly expanded braincase.

He turned the skull over. About a third of the posterior region was missing, but enough remained to reveal a primitive face, a high forehead, and a rounded cranial vault indicating a surprisingly large brain size for a human 1.5 million years old.

The anterior teeth were missing, as was the left side of the maxilla. The right maxilla was intact, except the teeth were nearly sheared off. Enough of the base of the molars was preserved, however, to indicate their relatively small size and square shape. The left side of the face was crushed. No matter, it could be restored. Portions of the cranium—the nasal area, brain case, temporal region, and eye orbits—were impregnated with hardened sand.

Then he remembered what led him there in the first place. From his day pack he removed the small box wrapped in rubber bands and retrieved the partial jaw he had removed from Slater's collection just four days ago. He turned the cranium over to a cavity where the left jaw had broken off from the rest of the maxilla. It was partially filled with sand, which he carefully scraped away with a penknife. He then slowly placed the "pig" fragment where it should go.

It fit perfectly!

With the full maxilla largely in place, and what remained of the canines and incisors, the full parabolic shape of the upper jaw was revealed. He turned the skull over and over looking at it from every angle. Enough of the basic elements were there. It was abundantly clear: early *Homo*, and not *sapiens*.

"Incredible!"

Could it be *Homo erectus*? No, there were differences. The overall aspect of the face was robust, yet the shape and size of the brain case looked more like modern humans.

This one was different, surprisingly large. Something new. It had to be. After all, the ancestors of this early traveler trekked to the New World from two continents away. No doubt about it. This skull was a new species. He would name it *Homo americanus*.

After digesting the magnitude of his discovery, Wilde abruptly jumped up and screamed into the empty desert, "I am the greatest!"

Chapter 11

Russell

At four in the afternoon, Wilde was ready to load up. He emptied the ice chest, wiped it dry, then carefully packed the skull with newspaper, using a stack of the bilingual *Presidio International* he had picked up that morning. What foresight! Then he paused, thought for a moment, and unwrapped the skull. He removed the jaw fragment and put it back in the small box inside his jacket.

Using a safety belt, he secured the ice chest to the back seat of the Land Rover, got behind the wheel and headed for Presidio, feeling like he had just won the Power Ball lottery. His mind raced. He knew he needed an expert to independently verify the context and location of the skull. Craig Russell was the only one he would trust. But he had to be careful since Russell, like himself, was on Slater's Ph.D. committee.

He had to get Russell.

He removed his cell phone from his pack and called Russell's home number. He was almost always there on Sundays with Linda and the kids. The phone rang and rang. "Answer the damn phone."

On the fifth ring a voice answered, "Hel—oops!"

Wilde heard the receiver crash to the floor . . . followed by fumbling around sounds.

"Oh great, it's the three-year-old boy."

"Hel—loops." Again, the receiver crashed to the floor. More fumbling around.

"Jesus!" Wilde fumed.

Finally, "Helloooh."

"Hello to you too!" Wilde responded, "Is this the village imbecile speaking?"

He could hear the kid's breathing and adenoidal drooling. He probably had the phone in his mouth flooding the circuits. "Is your father home?"

"Nope, he's at the . . ."

Suddenly, Wilde heard someone burst into the room, "Danny, I'll get that!" It was Russell's wife, Linda. He could imagine her wearing slippers, a robe, and a head full of shampoo.

"Where's your father?" Wilde quickly demanded.

"At the office."

Linda grabbed the phone, "Hello, this is Linda, who is this?"

The phone went dead.

CRCRCR

Russell sat at his computer in his cluttered office trying to catch up on his emails. A battered plaster cast of the *Zinjanthropus* skull, Mary Leakey's great discovery, hung suspended from the ceiling attached to a piece of wire, slowly twisting back and forth in sync with the air currents of the heating system. The phone rang.

Russell's golden retriever, Hazel, sprawled out asleep among piles of books and journals on the floor, jerked her head up, looked around—saw nothing dangerous on the horizon—then flopped back down. Russell looked at his Caller ID. Wilde, damn it. He ignored the ringing until it stopped; then it started up again. Wilde must have called his home first and somebody squealed on him. Probably Daniel. How was he going to teach that kid to lie? Now Melinda, his seven-year-old, would say he went to Chuck E Cheese for Christmas if he asked her. "Sure Dad. Chuck E Cheese. Can I go too?"

Reluctantly, Russell picked up the telephone as he looked out of his office window from the second floor of the Anthropology Building. The live oak trees stood gray and a light drizzle fell on the courtyard. Two Asian students bundled against the cold walked by in animated conversation. A flock of brown and white pigeons swept across his view.

"Hello Bert. What's up?"

"Craig, thank God I caught you! I'm near Presidio and I need your help, badly."

"Presidio? What the hell are you doing there?"

"I've made a discovery. I mean a dis-cov-er-ee!"

"I thought you were going to Bell County to rob old man Schultz of his Clovis site?"

"Nah, at the last minute, I thought of a better way to spend my time."

"So, what's up in Presidio?" Russell asked.

"The only thing I can say right now is that I've found something *very* significant among some early Pleistocene fossils. Can you spare a couple of days and come down here to help me out?"

"A couple of days? You're not serious."

"Craig, I'm more serious than I've ever been in my life. I've made a great discovery," Wilde said solemnly.

"You said 'early' Pleistocene fossils, near Presidio? You mean those that Ron Slater found? So, you think he's found something . . ."

"Hell no, forget Slater! He wouldn't know his dick from a duck. I'll tell you about that later."

"I thought he was your best graduate stu . . ."

"I said forget Slater! I've found something that's supernova material. I mean bigger than the Taung skull. Do you want to be part of it or not?"

Hardly, thought Russell. It was unlikely that he had found anything remotely as significant as Taung. Discovered in South Africa in 1924, the "man-ape" was the first discovery of its kind. Named *Australopithecus africanus*, "the southern ape of Africa," the skull had set off a revolution in knowledge of human origins.

"Bert, I can't just drop everything and drive off into the desert. It's Christmas time, I've got a conference to prepare for, the new semester coming up . . ."

"Craig, if it wasn't urgent I wouldn't be chatting with you in this moonscape surrounded by Mexicans sporting machetes. Look, I need an independent expert with me to document this find. This is too important. Trust me, you won't be disappointed. Come down for one day, that's all I ask. You'll be co-discoverer and famous."

That's a laugh! thought Russell. Wilde was not known to share anything with anybody, especially a discovery that stood a chance of attracting the media. Russell had struck his own fame early, in 1992, while exploring for fossils in central Turkey as part of his doctoral research at Yale. He found a 16 million-year-old ape skull, which he named *Ottomapithecus*, and identified as a precursor to the great apes, among them the chimpanzees, our nearest quadrupedal ancestors. After coming to the University of Texas, Russell and his students found more fossil beds in Turkey containing ape remains both older and slightly younger than *Ottomapithecus*, filling in yet more gaps in our hominoid ancestry.

Russell could only guess that Wilde found something pre-Clovis, or more likely Clovis with human remains. Either one would be a great discovery. But Wilde had said "early" Pleistocene. Russell was intrigued. He was a scientist to the core and, he liked to think, a student of aberrant primate behavior. He was just curious enough about Wilde's claim, and Wilde, to agree to go to West Texas for a three-day trip. After talking it over with Linda and sorting through their holiday obligations, Russell agreed to meet Wilde in Presidio late the following afternoon, Monday, and go see the "discovery" early Tuesday. That would put him back in Austin two days before Christmas. One day later and Linda would pull out his fingernails.

"Great! I promise you won't be disappointed."

It had taken Slater nearly two months to find his site. Russell couldn't believe Wilde had found another site in the few days he had been away. More likely, he was living up to his reputation for claim-jumping the hard-won efforts of others. The fossils Slater had collected were interesting, but important enough for Wilde to wet his pants over?

Russell didn't think so. Perhaps he found a coelacanth washed up on the shores of the Rio Grande.

C3C3C3

It was twilight by the time Wilde returned to Presidio. With darkness closing in and a dust storm brewing, the sky was a brilliant collage of orange, red, and crimson colors. He stopped at the El Patio Café and grabbed a double order of green enchiladas, while seated next to a window with his vehicle in full view. He took no chances on losing the skull, or having his Land Rover dismantled in a chop shop across the border. After paying his check, he headed back to the Three Palms Motel and put the ice chest in a closet. Then he called his female companion of the previous evening for another rendezvous.

As night fell, it was cold and windy outside. Sand grains pelted the windows sounding like static from an old radio. Sipping scotch from a plastic cup, Wilde paced the floor waiting for her.

"What a perfect way to celebrate one of the greatest scientific discoveries of all time!"

At eight o'clock sharp, as agreed, there was a light knock at his door.

C3C3C3

Russell arrived late the next afternoon and the two of them headed for the Scorpion Arroyo the following morning. They took Wilde's vehicle, allowing Russell the opportunity of leisurely looking over the countryside and the results of the prolonged drought. The Rio Grande Valley would normally look like a sparsely vegetated semi-desert, except for patches of greenbelt and farmland filling the meanders on either side of the river. Now, as they drove northwest, he could see that the landscape was nearly denuded, like it was struggling to overcome the effects of napalm. To the northeast, the Cienega Mountains were masked in a dull gray sheen in their lower reaches, against the glowing backdrop of sunrise. Stalks of *ocotillo* and *lechuguilla* marked the skyline, serving as way-stops for cowbirds and passerines. A prairie falcon swooped into a ravine closing in on a morning meal.

Before long, Wilde turned onto a ranch road and drove up to a cattle guard and an unlocked gate with a modest sign on it reading Double-H Ranch. After jumping out to open the gate, Russell asked what Double-H stood for.

"Probably Harrington and Harrington. Two brothers own the land the site is on."

"Do you know them?"

"Unfortunately," Wilde said, recalling their visit to the lab.

"Why do you say that?"

"They're just annoying, a little strange."

"But they gave Slater and you permission to work on their ranch?"

"Okay, here's the turnoff we want."

After driving eastward five or six miles on a dusty, bumpy road, Wilde parked the Land Rover behind the same hill he had parked behind the previous day.

The two of them grabbed their daypacks off the backseat. Wilde opened the lift gate and retrieved an ice chest, which Russell assumed contained cold drinks. Wilde then led them over to the plateau next to Scorpion Arroyo, where Slater's test pits were hidden by brush. After taking it all in, Russell was greatly impressed by Slater's ingenuity.

"I'm impressed! Finding and uncovering a bone bed beneath a blanket of gravel that probably stretches for miles is one hellava feat! So this is where Slater found all those fossils?"

Wilde said nothing. He didn't need to. Russell knew immediately that this was not his work. An exception was random potholes dug here and there, including one enlarged pit that looked like it had been attacked by a badger.

"Remarkable. Slater has done an extraordinary job here. Amazing," Russell offered.

"Not so fast," Wilde replied. "Recall that hominid maxilla we scanned a few days back?"

"Yes, of course," Russell replied.

"Well, I found that jaw in Slater's collection of fossils. He identified it as a *pig*. Can you believe that?"

"He's not the first to confuse the two, but what's that got to do with this site? That was an African hominid."

"You're not hearing me!" Wilde yelled.

"What do you mean, I'm not hearing you? What are you trying to tell me?" Russell suddenly became cautious and agitated. What Wilde was telling him made no sense.

"I'm sorry, but until I knew the jaw was genuine, I misled you. That fossil came from the very site you're standing on, which both you and Slater agree is approximately 1.5 million years old."

82

"Get real. I don't know where you got that jaw, but it damn sure didn't come from this hemisphere."

"Is that so? Just wait here."

Wilde left Russell standing where he was and without a word, walked over to test pit C carrying the ice chest, which he set down. After clearing away brush from the far end of the pit, he opened the chest and removed the skull wrapped in newspapers. With his back turned to Russell, he unwrapped it and carefully placed it in an excavated area next to the gravel.

Stepping back, Wilde said, "That's exactly where I found it."

"Found what?"

"See for yourself."

Russell slowly walked forward and knelt down. He started to reach for the fossil, then hesitated, staring at it—it was a skull. "What the hell?"

After a moment, he reached over and picked it up. Even though much of the skull was encrusted with sandstone, and partially crushed, he had no doubt what he was looking at. "Are you trying to tell me that this fossil came from here?" He stabbed his finger at the ground.

"Correct," Wilde smiled.

"That's ridiculous. Slater and several others, including myself, are convinced this assemblage is early Pleistocene, about 1.5 million, and you and I both know this fossil has *Homo* written all over it. And by the way, we happen to be in North America, not Africa!"

"Look Craig, I'm not trying to convince you of anything. As I said, you can see for yourself. That's why I asked you to come here as an independent expert."

"Okay, then." Russell pointed to the ice chest. "As an independent expert I saw you take that fossil out of that box and plant it in the ground."

"Of course! I found the skull two days ago. You don't think I'd leave it out here do you, especially with wetbacks watching me?"

"Wetbacks?"

"Hell yes, they're all over the place. And by the way, when I called you Sunday on my cell phone, I had *just* found the skull. You were the first and only person I called."

Wilde then reached into his jacket pocket and pulled out the small specimen box. He unwrapped the partial jaw and handed it to Russell. "Remember this?"

"Sure, I remember it."

"Go head—see if it fits."

Still holding the skull, Russell sat down and slowly placed the jaw fragment in the cavity of the maxilla where it obviously came from. The fit was solid. He could clearly see the configuration of the cheek teeth on either side of the palate. When the canines are prominent, as in apes and many non-primates, the cheek teeth form a U-shaped dental arc. With the reduction of canines, as in the genus *Homo*, the dentition results in a parabolic arc.

"Does it fit?" Wilde asked.

Russell carefully looked at the match-up. "Oh yes."

"Okay," said Wilde, as he gently took the fragment and skull back from Russell. "Then let's reunite this baby with its mother-ship." He removed a tube of Ducco cement from his pack, blew dust from the fragment and the cavity in the skull, and applied a few drops of cement to the area of contact. He then inserted the fragment into its obvious place of origin and waited for the glue to dry. Later, acetone would easily dissolve the glue so the fragment could be removed when it came time to thoroughly clean the cranium.

Wilde handed the skull back to Russell, "Look okay?"

"Yes. Yes!" Russell quickly responded, although in fact he was deeply troubled. "I can't believe I'm sitting here watching you casually glue two pieces of bone together on what could be one of the greatest paleoanthropological discoveries ever. This is bizarre. This is impossible!"

"What's impossible?" asked Wilde.

"This whole thing is impossible! This skull flies in the face of everything we know about human origins in North America. One-and-a-half million years old. *No one* will believe it."

"Don't worry, we'll analyze this thing to death! The CT scans of the jaw were convincing, right?"

"Yes, we've been through that," Russell replied.

"Then what's troubling you about the rest of the skull?"

"Take a guess!" Russell blurted out. "This isn't exactly your run-of-the-mill discovery. This is quantum science we've got here and I'm not talking about electrons."

"You think I don't know that?" Wilde said. "You think I don't know this is the find of the century! Look Craig, let's calm down and see what we've got here. How about we discuss human migrations during the early Pleistocene, because there are some new data that . . ."

"No! Let's backup and review how we got to this site

in the first place. If I'm supposed to be the expert witness, I want to know everything."

"Okay, let's review whatever you like." But Wilde thought, *who the hell does this* guy *think he is*?

"You say you first saw the jaw fragment in Slater's collection at the VP Lab?"

"Correct," said Wilde evenly, "five days ago."

"Was anyone else with you?"

"Of course, Slater and the owners of this ranch, the Harringtons, who we invited to visit the lab and see the collections."

"What did Slater say about all this?"

"About what?"

"The hominid jaw."

"Not a goddamned thing. As I told you, he identified the jaw as pig and I wasn't about to make a fool out of myself or him and say, 'Excuse me, but this specimen actually came from the moon' until we had some lab work done. That's when we had the jaw scanned and compared it to casts of *Homo*. After that, I came out here and on a long shot found the rest of the cranium."

"Using Slater's maps and report on the site."

Wilde turned red in the face, "That's right! Slater is in Arizona for the holidays. Would you expect me to just sit around with the possibility of a discovery of this magnitude just waiting to be found?"

"Well, you might have waited long enough to call Slater at his home, Tucson, I believe."

"Get real! You know as well as I do that finding the rest of the skull was a stroke of blind luck."

"Yes, but . . ."

"But nothing!" Wilde tried to control himself.

Russell knew he wasn't going to win this argument. He'd go to the dean of graduate research, or the president of the university, if necessary, to make sure Slater got full credit for finding the site and the hominid jaw. After all, he had just begun studying the collection, and as bright as Slater was, it wouldn't have taken him long to recognize his mistake.

"Look," said Wilde, "I know exactly what you're saying. Slater will get full credit for everything he should get credit for, as of course, will you. I suggest the schedule now is to relax over the holidays, think about what we've found, and wait until Slater gets back. After he cleans and restores the skull, we can write it up and fire off a paper to *Scien*ce, with Slater as senior author."

"That's what I was waiting to hear," said Russell. "We'll play it by the book."

"By the book. Now, how about we take a few minutes to discuss who this fossil is and how it arrived in this hemisphere 1.5 million years before Columbus."

They sat on the edge of the pit and discussed the skull's morphology feature by feature, while carefully handing it back and forth to refer to one point or another. Wilde had already formed his opinion on the skull. It was a new species of *Homo*.

Russell immediately concurred. "*Homo* for sure, but unlike any I have seen."

"Agreed," Wilde offered. "And don't you think the face is somewhere between *erectus* and its more gracile successors? It's not early *sapiens,* but the high forehead and enlarged braincase are comparable."

"Altogether," Russell conjectured, "I'd guess this hominid shared a common ancestor with *erectus*, then went its separate way in the early Pleistocene. The timing fits, if we're right about the 1.5 million-year-old age of this fossil. It's almost as if a population of *erectus* from Africa made it as far as Central Asia, then split: one group went southeast eventually reaching Java; the other ventured northeast deep into Asia, where a shift in climate left them trapped in the Siberian deep freeze.

"Somehow this group used its wits to survive the cold and crossed over to the New World on the Beringian land bridge," Russell continued. "Perhaps the demands of the northern environment favored robust, cold-adapted humans with greater intelligence. Whatever the circumstances, we're certainly dealing with a new species. That's about the best I can offer right now."

"Very good," said Wilde, "but it's the 'survive the cold' part that worries me. Temperatures around the Bering Strait during the Ice Ages are estimated to have reached 40 to 60 degrees below zero. Any animal crossing the land bridge at that time, besides woolly mammoths and yaks, would need Gortex clothing and battery-heated boots. On the other hand, there are some significant new data you should know about."

He then told Russell about "a report" he had read describing the tectonic uplift of Beringia during a warm period in the early Pleistocene, between about 1.6 and 1.4 million years ago. "This could serve as our working model for the early migration of humans into North America."

"Nice, very nice!" exclaimed Russell. "Can you give me that report or citation when we get back to Austin?"

"Of course."

"So what happened to these early humans after they got here that caused their extinction?" Russell asked.

"That's a good question. You can bet this discovery will cause a stampede of paleoanthropologists into early Pleistocene fossil beds on this continent looking for answers, and more fossils."

After taking numerous pictures of the skull, the site and spot where it was found, the stratigraphy in the arroyo, and Wilde holding the skull, the two of them threw the brush back over the pit and Wilde repacked the skull in the ice chest. On their way back to Presidio, Russell wanted to again raise the issue that they had preempted Slater's work, but then thought the better of it. *There will be plenty of time to do this. For now, it's best to part on good terms.*

By late afternoon they had made it back to Presidio and hurried through an early dinner. Both felt they should head back to Austin right away instead of staying the night as planned. As they parted, Russell suggested they run a CT scan of the rest of the skull as soon as possible, to get some indication of its brain size.

"Sure, but let's get through Christmas first."

"Agreed."

It was a long drive back to Austin. Russell made it halfway, as far as Ozona, before stopping for the night. Wilde drove straight through arriving in Austin at midnight. He had work to do, starting *now*. He knew the media would go crazy with this one!

Chapter 12

Pistola Amigo

On the day of Wilde's "discovery" Slater found himself hiking along Chinati Creek down from the hot springs. He had looked forward to this Christmas break and would make up his absence from his family in Tucson at the first opportunity. Considering his traumatic year, he wanted to avoid the probing questions about his personal life and career goals that he knew people would be asking him.

Slater was only one of three visitors at the springs that day and the only camper. The other two guests were a young couple who spent their time secluded in one of the adobe cabins, only to surface now and then to soak in the large outdoor hot tub.

In the late afternoon, Slater sat on the tailgate of his pickup truck peeling a potato and slicing up vegetables for his dinner, when Rocío came speeding down the graded road leading to the campsite on her Honda motorbike. Slater had been expecting her since he knew that Chihuahua University had just let out for Christmas break. She skidded to a stop in a cloud of dust in front of him and turned off the engine.

"Ronaldo, you're back and saved!"

"I told you I would be here for the holidays. What do you mean, I'm 'saved'? From what?"

"Ronaldo, I went by your *fosíles* place this morning thinking you could be there and instead there was this bad man, *muy malo*, there digging in your places and when he saw me he stood up and called me bad names, like *puta* and wetback, and pointed a *pistola* at me and told me to leave or he would kill me *muerta*. He chased me until I escaped. Do you know this man, Ronaldo? I was worried he had done something, like killed you! He said he was with the Border Patrol, but his vehicle was gray with a University of Texas parking permit on it. I didn't believe him."

"What did he look like?"

"*Muy grande*, very big and tall, *con mucho pelo rojo*."

"Red hair. Was he alone?"

"*Sí.*"

"I know him, and you're right, he's not with the Border Patrol. He's a bad man. We mustn't go near him."

"Oh, he's already gone. I watched him through my binoculars until he left about two hours ago. *Porque* is he a bad man?"

"I don't know. He just is."

"What are you going to do now? If that man is *peligroso* you cannot go back there. He might come back and shoot you."

"I don't intend to go back there. I've been invited to visit the Chase Ranch north of here, for a week. Very old fossils have been found there and the geology is said to be spectacular . . ."

"Well! That's wonderful for you, Ronaldo. I hope you have a *maravilloso* time while I'm left behind to defend myself from your *pistola amigo* who tried to kill me."

"Of course you're invited to join me. I was getting to that."

"It doesn't matter what you were getting to. You go and enjoy yourself. But you might be interested that my Uncle Fernando's *rancho* is directly across the Rio Grande from the *rancho* Chase, and I have been there *muchas veces* and know the whole *familia*. We are very good friends. But it doesn't matter because my parents don't know you and your *pistola amigo* and would never let me go with a *gringo* anyway."

"Wait a minute. I'd love for you to join me. I was going to invite you because . . ."

"Because what?"

"Because, I'd like you to join me."

Rocio looked at the potato Slater was holding, "What are you going to do with that potato?" All the time they were talking Slater was peeling and slicing up vegetables.

"I'm making dinner."

"For just one person?"

CBCBCB

First thing in the morning after arriving in Austin from Presidio, Wilde made some phone calls from his study. Alice was just leaving to run some errands. They hadn't exchanged five words since he pulled into the driveway at midnight, although she was in a good mood as she puttered around the house. If she only knew that he had spent the previous two evenings with a sex goddess.

Wilde scrolled through the names in his email

directory. The first person he called was Brad Roberts, Dean of Liberal Arts, at his home in Northwest Hills. "Brad, I know you're about to head out for some last minute Christmas shopping, but I wanted you to be the first to know about my latest discovery."

"Oh? In Africa?"

"No, in the Rio Grande Valley, where I've shifted my interest."

"The Valley? Hey, that's where I'm from! I grew up in Harlingen. Did you know it's the state's richest agricultural area?"

"Harlingen?"

"For openers, we're number one in citrus fruit production. So, what the heck did you find down there?"

"Actually, Brad, my discovery came from higher up the valley, near Presidio."

"From Presidio, God forbid! What the heck did you find there? Darn sure wasn't rain."

Wilde then told him about the human skull he found and its age.

"Whoa, that's a whopper of a discovery! A 1.5 million-year-old human skull in North America. Texas, in fact." The dean, a stout man with short hair and long, trimmed sideburns, who was wearing ostrich skin cowboy boots, knew something about human origins from years of reading articles about hominid discoveries in *Scientific American* and *National Geographic*. Dean Roberts also proved an important link in the rapid approval of Wilde's appointment in May.

"Initially, I put a graduate student on the site," Wilde continued. "But after he identified a hominid jaw as a pig, as if pigs and humans were related, I figured I'd better look at the site myself. That's when I discovered the skull."

"Amazing. This student doesn't sound too swift."

"Actually, he's very bright. He's not the first person to confuse a pig with a hominid. Even Louis Leakey made that mistake on one occasion."

"Amazing. You move fast for someone who just got here. May, wasn't it?"

"Yes, Brad, fortunately for me." Wilde detected nothing in his voice to suggest the dean had picked up on his problems with NSF and Harvard.

"Was the student with you when you made the find?"

"No, Craig Russell in the Department of Anthro . . ."

"I know who Craig is."

"Of course. He joined me in the field and verified the skull's location and geological context. In fact, Craig has already completed a CT scan of part of the cranium in the Computed Tomography Labora . . ."

"I know where CT scans are made."

"Certainly . . . and with excellent results." Dean Roberts was starting to get on Wilde's nerves.

"So, how the heck did humans get over here back then, by canoe? Or did they walk across a land bridge during the Ice Ages?"

"In the late Pleistocene they probably used both methods, but important new data indicates that in the early Pleistocene, Beringia was subjected to tectonic uplift during a temperate period. Pollen in cores obtained from offshore drilling has revealed that approximately 1.5 million years ago, uplift of the sea floor across the strait turned Beringia into a forested land bridge."

"During a warming period, you say?"

"Exactly. Of course the idea that humans may have crossed that early is only conjecture, but the Beringia tectonic model gives us something to go on."

"Good, something to go on, a working model. I like that. So where do you go from here, fire off a paper to *Science*?"

"That's our thinking, but frankly speaking, I'm worried about something, Brad, and I was hoping for some guidance from you."

"What's that?"

"Well, when I was excavating the skull, I spotted some people spying on me. I can't prove it, but knowing how unprincipled some paleoanthropologists are, I'm afraid another university may want to beat us to the punch."

"Claim-jump our site?"

"Believe me, I've seen it happen."

"Son of a gun!"

"Unfortunately, it's possible they could find more of the hominid, like the lower jaw or post-cranial bones, which are still missing. They could even contact journalists to claim discovery of the site, and before you know it, *their* discovery is featured on the cover of *Time*."

"You mean they could scoop us?"

"Like I said, I've seen it happen before, Brad."

"Well, we darn sure don't want that to happen, especially a discovery of this magnitude! In fact, maybe we can beat them at their own game. Let me try to reach Cassie Burgess, since the dean of graduate research should be in on this from the beginning. I'll get back to you in fifteen minutes or so."

Instead of Dean Roberts calling Wilde back, however, Dean Burgess herself called twelve minutes later. She was on her mountain bike on the hike and bike trail between Enfield Drive and Lake Austin Boulevard, wearing a headset connected to her cell phone. It was a brilliant sunny morning in the low 60s. A woman's woman, Cassie did a hundred sit-ups and fifty push-ups every morning, which kept her in shape for the succession of girlfriends who visited her home in Tarrytown.

She was breathing hard, "Hey Bert, Cassie here, *huf, huf*, sounds like you hit a Big One in the Rio Grande Valley! Unbelievable. Congratulations, *huf, huf, huf*. Can't wait to see it."

"Thanks. You must be on your bike again."

"Yeah, despite the jerks hogging the trail. Brad briefed me on the competition problem at your site and we're both, *huf, huf, huf*, concerned that others may not . . . *Get out of the way, idiot!* . . . be respectful of the priority of your find. You know that science ethics . . . *Up yours, asshole!* . . . is one of my concerns, *huf, huf*."

"That's good to hear."

"Brad and I think a press conference, *huf, huf*, is in order right after Christmas. How does that sound to you?"

"I hadn't thought of that at this point, but that would seal the find for the university. I could return to Presidio tomorrow and protect the site until the press conference."

"Spend Christmas away from your gorgeous wife? You must feel, *huf, huf, huf*, the competition is pretty threatening if you're willing to make that kind of sacrifice. She's a real looker, by the way."

"Yes, well, Cassie, I know from my work in Africa

that discovery of an early hominid brings a lot of prestige, and grant money, to an institution. I can only guess what a 1.5 million-year-old human skull found in Texas would generate."

"Say no more, *huf, huf, huf,* I hear you. Let me talk this over—hang on, Bert. I'm stopping for water—*slurrrrp, slurrrrp, slurrrrp*—with Eric Dietz, because the president should be informed of this find right away. I have something in mind that will require his approval. I'll get back to you as soon as I reach him. Meanwhile, it would be useful if you drew up a brief memo outlining a short history of the discovery, its significance, how you found the site, others involved, who owns the land, and so forth, and email that to Dietz, Dean Roberts, and myself. Nothing fancy, a page or two."

" . . . sure, Cassie, no problem."

"By the way, I was at an NSF meeting recently and one of their people mentioned to me, in confidence, something about a problem you had with the foundation?"

Caught off guard, Wilde replied, "Yes . . . ah, but that's history now."

"Something about a continuing award to you that was *withdrawn*. Can that be true?"

"As I said, that was Harvard-related."

"Perhaps if you sent me a memo . . . "

Now very irritated, Wilde replied, "Cassie, we can go over anything you like, but right now is not a good time."

"Of course. I'm sorry. I know you have a lot on your mind. I'll call President Dietz about the press conference this minute and call you back."

"Thanks." Wilde hung up. "The nosy bitch!"

Chapter 13

Rocío

President Dietz himself called twenty minutes later.

"Bert, I heard the whole story from Cassie and Brad. I won't waste words. Your discovery is remarkable. Congratulations."

"Thanks, Eric, I appreciate that."

"It's the kind of thing that will impress the hell out of the Board of Regents. And moneyed alumni. Maybe even get that wing added to the Anthropology Building that's been kicked around for decades."

"That would make my colleagues and me very happy."

President Dietz had spent most of his career with NASA and only recently joined academia. His numerous appearances before appropriation committees for the space program had given him a well-deserved reputation as a fund-raiser.

"In fact, Bert, this skull is the most exciting discovery I've heard about on this planet in years. Hell, in the entire solar system. Imagine, humans in the Western Hemisphere over a million years ago."

"Yes, it's truly amazing. But let's cut to the chase, Bert. I'm very concerned about Texas A&M sniffing around our site like I heard from Dean Roberts. I know something about competition and we don't want another Sputnik. There's no glory coming in second. All things considered, we should go with this right away."

"Go with . . .?"

"Yes, a full press conference. The TV networks, the press, everybody. I'll light a fire under the PR director and his staff of beauty queens, I don't care how close we are to Christmas."

"Sounds good to me, Eric. When do you want to go with this?"

"Let's launch this baby right away. We'll schedule the press conference for the day after tomorrow at ten hundred in Batts Hall. That work with you?"

"That would be great."

"Good. I'll give you an introduction. You show the skull to the media and discuss its significance, then we'll have a brief Q&A. Roberts said you had a UT colleague who helped document the discovery, correct?"

"Yes, Craig Russell in anthro . . ."

"Bring him along for the Q&A. We'll keep it to about one hour. This should make a terrific splash on the mid-day and evening news. I'm sure we'll have the media crawling all over us for months. This will be a PR blast-off if there ever was one."

 CRCRCR

For five days Slater and Rocío hiked and climbed over the Chase Ranch, from the towering eastern margins of the Rio Grande rift, to the white, red, and coralline tuffaceous strata on the floor of the rift. Slater's invitation to visit the ranch was made possible by a telephone call from Ernest Wilkins, professor emeritus at UT, to the ranch's owner, John Chase.

Throughout the 1950s Wilkins and a succession of graduate students had braved the heat during the summer months on the Chase Ranch, and on neighboring ranches, mapping the complex geology of the heavily faulted terrain west of the Sierra Vieja. Vertebrate fossils of numerous extinct mammals were found that included a 37 million-year-old tarsier-like prosimian, which Wilkins named *Rooneyia viajaensis*, after the mountain range and Sheriff Rooney of Presidio County, who had introduced Wilkins to the ranchers in the region.

At the end of each day Slater was exhausted, not just physically, but from Rocío's relentless questions. She didn't limit her questions to geology and paleontology, but she wanted to know what he thought of Bill Clinton, Monica, NAFTA, the destruction of the rain forests, the possibility of life on Mars . . .

"Ronaldo, how come you don't say anything about *su familia*? Do you have brothers and sisters? A girlfriend?"

"Of course I do, lots, one of each."

Rocío was silent for a moment, "One of each of what, a brother and sister?"

"Yes, one of each of those, too."

"Girlfriends?"

"Sure, one in Presidio, Marfa, Bosnia . . ."

"Ronaldo, you're joking on me, I'm sure. Correct?"

Towards the end of their stay, Rocío asked, "Why go back to that *universidad* in *Tejas* when we have a great *universidad* in *Cuidad Chihuahua*? Also, I'm sure we have more *fósiles* in *Mejico*, because *Mejico* is *doble* the size of *Tejas*. And in Chihuahua you will learn *español* and not have to struggle with *inglés* all the time."

"Rocío, you've talked about Chihuahua University for days. You sound like a walking alumni association. How could I not think about it?"

"*Bien*, so that means you have been thinking about it?"

છpreviouslyછછ

Because the weather was dry and cool and not overly cold in the late night, unusually so for late December when temperatures can drop below freezing, Slater and Rocío simply slept wherever they wanted, as long as the ground was relatively flat and smooth. The Chases loaned Rocío an extra bedroll, an air mattress, a pillow, a ground tarp, and a plastic cover for protection from the morning dew.

Slater had adequate food and water, which he kept in his pickup truck as they moved camp from place to place, exploring deeper and deeper into the 32,000-acre ranch. They basked in the sun in the middle of the day when they had lunch, and on one occasion camped near some warm springs for bathing at the end of the day, although they did so separately and discretely, until their fourth night.

They had walked far that day and did not arrive back at camp until after sundown. By the time they reached the nearby springs, which formed a waist-deep pool at the base of a cliff, it was fully dark. They were acutely aware of each other's presence as they took off their clothes and stepped into the warm water at the same time.

In an instant they both shouted out and fell against each other as one or both slipped on a thin clay layer covering the smooth rock floor of the pool. Before they could think about it, they had fallen into the water and into each other's arms laughing and splashing.

Later, after they changed into clean clothes and shared a meal of chorizo, potatoes, and *jalapeños* wrapped in tortillas, they propped their sore feet near the fire and sipped hot tea sweetened with mesquite honey.

The air temperature was in the low sixties, but dropping rapidly as they huddled side-by-side covered in their bedrolls. Slater chose that time to tell Rocío his story, about Laura, Harvard, and the "*pistola* man." Rocío didn't say a word, but when he finished she leaned over and kissed him on the lips, and they embraced for the longest time. They talked well into the night, long after the last coals of the fire burned out and sank into ashes.

Chapter 14

Beringia

Batts Hall was starting to fill. As planned, the press conference was scheduled for 10:00 a.m. with 30 minutes to go. The PR people had done their job well. Scores of journalists from all over the country, and a number of foreign correspondents, milled about. TV cameras from the major networks were setting up and photographers jockeyed for a good view of the stage.

The buzz foretold something monumental was to be announced, an "epic" discovery. For suspense, the university kept the nature of the find under wraps until the appointed hour. Certainly, no university in the country would hold a press conference three days before Christmas unless something extraordinary was to be revealed. A brief press release referred to "a discovery of such magnitude that it would change our thinking of humanity forever." One journalist quipped, "Gosh, that sounds like my writing!" Another speculated that it was some "thing" from outer space. After all, before his appointment as UT president, and while at NASA, Eric Dietz was an outspoken supporter of the SETI and the Life on Mars programs. When Bert Wilde's name was leaked as associated with the discovery, those who covered the fossil hominid beat immediately assumed it was another African find. On this one, a university spokeswoman broke the code of silence to a group of journalists. Tossing her head back, she pronounced, emphatically, that the announcement had *nothing to do with Africa.*"

Russell only learned about the planned press conference the night before, after he and Linda returned to their Travis Heights home from Christmas shopping. After picking up their kids at a neighbor's house and getting them to bed, Russell finally got around to listening to his telephone messages at 10:15.

He was dumbstruck to hear, "Message 5, today, 6:27 p.m.," from Wilde, telling him that a press conference announcing the discovery was scheduled for eleven the next morning at Batts Hall. "Craig, I know it's a shocker, but Dean Roberts called on other business and then asked what I was up to over the holidays. I couldn't lie to him. When I told him about the skull, he freaked out. It turns out he's from the Rio Grande Valley and he takes this find personally. He went straight to President Dietz, who jumped on it as well, insisting we take it to the media right away. I've tried to reach Slater at his home in Tucson and I've left messages everywhere. I'm sure he'll turn up. Anyway, if you would be prepared to talk about the Beringia thing during the Q&A that would be great, at least that's what Dietz suggested. I slipped Slater's report about it under your office door. Remember: Batts Hall, 11:00 a.m. See you there."

"Press conference? The "Beringia thing?" Dietz wants me to discuss the Beringia thing at a press conference!

What goddamn *Beringia thing*? He recalled that Wilde had mentioned "a report" about the uplift of Beringia during a warming period as a possible explanation for the migration of early *Homo* into North America, but he didn't say it was an unpublished report by a graduate student!

Russell immediately called Slater's telephone number, in the event he was still in Austin. He was not surprised there was no answer, but he was very surprised to hear that his telephone line "has been disconnected."

It was then 9:20 p.m. Mountain Standard Time in Tucson where Wilde said Slater was spending the holidays with his family. He called Tucson information. There were a dozen or more Slaters listed.

After calling them one by one, finally Slater number eleven, the voice of an elderly man answered. "Yes, this is Ron's father and yes, he now goes to the University of Texas," he said, with some irritation in his voice. "What's this all about?"

After apologizing for the intrusion and identifying himself, Russell told him it was "nothing urgent, a matter of some research your son has done, much to his credit. Could I please speak with Ron, if he's there?"

Mr. Slater replied, "I'm sorry, but Ron is spending Christmas camping out in the *wilderness* somewhere. If you find him, tell him Merry Christmas from his *family*!"

Russell slept little that night. Wilde said he had "left messages everywhere" for Slater. Where? His father made no mention that Wilde had tried to reach him and, to his knowledge, Slater didn't carry a cell phone.

ଔଔଔଔ

Russell arrived at his office at 7:15 a.m. Wilde had slipped Slater's report under his door as he said he would. Russell carefully read through "Faunal migrations from Asia to North America: the evidence." There were numerous references and endnotes. However, he found only a few short paragraphs in the report about the tectonic uplift of Beringia, now their "working model" for the eastward migration of early humans. But the "model" fell woefully short of the kind of discussion one would expect for such an important finding. If he, Craig Russell, was to appear on stage before the world to discuss this "theory," at minimum he wanted to read Slater's primary sources. There were a number of references about the history of the land bridge in his report. However, only one purported to bear directly on tectonics of Beringia in the Pleistocene, published in the journal *PalaeoArctica* in 1997, with the unlikely title "Paleoflora of the Bering Strait in the Pleistocene."

Now Russell was very dubious about the accuracy of Slater's report, but nevertheless felt he couldn't just reject his findings out of hand. He turned on his computer.

As it started up, he looked outside and watched the ubiquitous ground squirrels and grackles hopping and running about. It looked like it would be a clear day, probably in the mid-40s. After the screen came on, he checked his email. Nothing from Slater, of course. He switched to UTNetCat to see if *PalaeoArctica* was on-line in the university library system. A bold message appeared on the screen saying the UT library computers were down for a holiday checkup. He grabbed his coat and jogged across the courtyard to see if by some miracle the geology building and its library were open. By luck, an elderly geology professor he had previously met was just unlocking the front door.

"Sure, I'll break a dozen rules and let an *anthropologist* into the building without notifying security. I'll even break more rules and let you in the library."

"That's very kind of you. Really sorry to be of trouble."

"Well, you should be, I have my reputation to look out for. Now, what do you study again?" his escort asked as he pushed the elevator button for the third floor. "Asian apes, as I recall?"

"That's it, fossil Asian apes."

"*Fossil* apes! That's too bad, because the state legislature here has quite a few living apes that need studying."

After letting him in the library, the professor said, "I've got a copy machine in my office if you need it. Just down the hall," pointing to the south end of the building. "It's an old one, but it's faster than a scribe."

Russell went straight to the display shelves where current issues of journals were arranged in alphabetical order. *PalaeoArctica* was not among them. *Damn.* He then went to the circulation desk and consulted the bound master list of all the journals scattered throughout the many UT libraries. To his relief, *PalaeoArctica* was kept in the Life Sciences Library in the Main Building. Also called the Tower, it was the highest building on the campus and home of the university's executive offices in the upper floors.

Russell looked at his watch. It was 8:32. Two and a

half hours before the press conference. He raced out of the Geology Building without even thanking his host.

"Typical anthropologist," he would say.

Chapter 15

Press Conference

Roper and Rider had just reached Johnson City, 35 miles from Austin, on their way back to West Texas. They had spent a week in the capital visiting "defectors," a brother and sister who had moved with their families from the purity of Presidio County to the "city of evil," the seat of the state government. Roper had just filled his 1986 Ford pickup with gas for the long trip back home, between listening to country music on KVET and arguing with Rider.

"You gotta be kidding," said Rider. "This rolling dump wouldn't get 25 miles to a gallon of gas even if it was downhill all the way to the border."

"I'll tell you what, if we don't make it to Fort Stockton on this tank, I'll buy you a five-course meal at the Dairy Queen."

"That's just my point. If we don't make it to Fort Stockton, there won't be a Dairy Queen."

Just then the nine o'clock news came on the radio. After listening to yet more revelations about President Clinton's sex life by Ken Starr and his semen team, came notice that "As the University of Texas announced

109

yesterday, a televised press conference will be held at ten o'clock this morning with news of a major scientific discovery, one that promises to be of great interest to all Texans. University officials refuse further comment. The event will . . ."

"Son of a bitch, that's got to—"

"Shut up, Rider!"

" . . . that's Batts Hall located just west of the UT Tower," the announcement concluded.

"Batts Hall, here we come!" Roper yelled. "Yihaaa!"

He made a screeching U-turn in the middle of the highway in front of an empty cattle truck that roared past the pickup with nine of its eighteen wheels on the shoulder of the road kicking up gravel, beer cans, burning rubber, and blasting its air-horn for a full ten seconds by one pissed-off trucker.

"Jesus, God almighty! What are you doing?" Rider screamed. "You damn near got us killed!"

"You know what that discovery is? It's those bones found on our ranch, pinhead. Remember the professor telling us those fossils are 'one of the greatest discoveries ever made in Texas'?"

"You think I don't know that, but I want to live to tell about it!"

"We'll do more than that. We'll make sure the world knows that the discovery was made on the Double-H. This is our chance to be on TV!" Roper looked at his watch. "It's fourteen minutes to nine, we can make it!"

"Right, 'we can make it,' or *die* trying!"

CROSCOS

Back in his office in the Anthropology Department, Russell called Wilde's home on the remote chance that he would be there before heading to Batts Hall. Just maybe he had heard something from Slater. To his surprise, the phone was answered on the first ring by a woman. "Peter?"

"No, this is Craig Russell. Is this Mrs. Wilde?" They had met at several social functions.

"Yes, this is Alice. How are you, Craig, and your family?"

"Very well. Actually Alice, I'm a bit out of sorts. Is Bert there by any chance?"

"No, he won't be back until well after the press conference, I am sure. Can I help?"

"No, probably not, unless Bert has mentioned anything about the whereabouts of Ron Slater, one of his graduate students?"

"I know quite a bit about that tragic young man, but almost nothing about the press conference."

"You said *tragic*?"

"I'm referring to the death of Laura Hudson."

"Laura?"

"His fiancée."

"*What*? I've heard nothing of this."

"She died in April, in Cambridge."

"How did she—?"

"I am sorry, Craig. I really must be going."

"My apologies. I just . . ."

The phone went dead.

Alice hung up the phone and continued packing.

Russell slowly put the telephone down and leaned back in his chair, staring at the chimpanzees loping across the

111

screen saver on his computer. Whatever anxieties he had about Slater just doubled. He had to think this through.

Slater had a fiancée while he was at Harvard, who died in April, just weeks before he came to Texas. Is this why he left Cambridge? To get away from this "tragic" event in his life? How did Laura die? Alice Wilde knew all about this, yet Bert never mentioned a word about it. Not that it was really any of his business, but still he thought Bert would have said something.

Russell looked at his wall clock. It was now 9:03 a.m., two hours before the press conference. He still had time to pursue "the Beringia model." He had one last chance. Knowing the Life Sciences Library would be locked, he called its head librarian, Sandra Mayer, at her home. A divorcee, he knew her well since they had mutual friends, and he frequently asked her to comb through databases for obscure sources.

"Good morning, Sandra, Craig Russell here. I hope I'm not intruding on your holiday of prayer and spending."

"I hope you're calling for a reprieve from your years of overdue books by taking me out for breakfast?"

"Actually, I've got a bit of an emergency."

"That's what they all say. What's up?"

He hurriedly explained he needed to see some critical data from the journal *PalaeoArctica* for a pending press conference. She knew of the journal and about the press conference.

"You actually have this journal in the library."

"*Excuse me*, UT happens to have the fourth largest university library in the country. Yes, we have the journal. What year?"

"1997."

"What do you want me to do? Run to the campus and check it out for you for Christmas?"

"Not exactly. I was hoping I could meet you there and briefly look at the journal, maybe copy a few pages. It's really important. It shouldn't take more than ten minutes."

Sensing the urgency in his voice, she agreed. "Okay, Craig, give me fifteen minutes to get there. I'll meet you at the west entrance. You can't miss me, I'll be the one in pajamas."

"Look, I'm really sorry."

"Fifteen minutes," she repeated and hung up. Fortunately, she lived in Hyde Park just north of the university.

Fourteen minutes later she showed up in a vintage Volvo. She parked near the entrance of the building and jumped out of the car wearing a purple turtleneck sweater, jeans, and tennis shoes without socks. Attractive, 40-ish, with thick, slightly graying black hair hastily swept back from her forehead.

"You owe me big time, buster!" she said, as she unlocked the outside door and they hurried into the building.

"Agreed. How about a box of Don's Donuts, the creamy kind?"

"Actually, I had something more in mind, like The Four Seasons."

Russell gave her the card catalog number for the journal he had copied down from the journal master list in the Geology Department.

She handed it back, "Don't bother, I know where the

journal is."

Once in the building, they hurried up the stairs to the library on the second floor. Sandra unlocked the door and led him inside. After flipping on a few light switches, she led him down a narrow flight of stairs into the cramped, poorly lit sub-basement known as the "catacombs" among the staff, where the open stacks were found.

Russell mused to himself, "And they call this the *Life* Sciences Library. It's said that every five or six years a librarian enters this part of the building never to be seen again."

Sandra quickly located the 1997 bound volume of *PalaeoArctica* and the article Russell wanted. Before handing it to him, she opened the front cover and found a slip of paper with some notations on it.

"I thought so. You're lucky."

"Why's that?"

"This volume just came back from the bindery a few days ago after being out of circulation for two months."

"That's odd," Russell said, looking at the December 15 date on Slater's research paper, which he had brought with him.

"Not at all, getting journals bound commonly takes up to two months."

"That's not what I meant. Over the past six weeks or so a graduate student wrote this research paper," which he handed to her. "The student refers to important data from this volume of *PalaeoArctica* when the journal wasn't even available in the library. This journal can't be on-line yet?"

"Not if you're holding it in your hands."

"I understand."

"But if the journal was at the bindery when he was researching his paper, he could have easily obtained a photocopy of the article through inter-library loan, although that can take several weeks."

"Right."

"Also, your student could have obtained the table of contents of the journal electronically, if all he wanted was author and title."

"Yes."

"But Craig, I'm sure you're not here because you're studying to be a librarian; also, you've already used up your fifteen minutes."

"Whoa!" he said looking at his watch, "I'll hustle."

"I'll give you fifteen more minutes. You can use that desk against the wall. I'll blink the lights when it's time to leave."

"Many thanks." As Russell sat down he briefly noted generations of initials carved on the top of the desk. He could make out the letters H-E-L-P. He wondered what ever happened to that student.

He flipped open the volume to the article about paleoflora in the Bering Strait in the Pleistocene. Authored jointly by researchers from the U.S. and Russia, the report was indeed about temperate climate and vegetation changes in Beringia. However, the time period covered was during a late Pleistocene interglacial warming episode, some 46,000 to 38,000 years ago. There was not a *word* in the article about a tectonic event 1.5 million years ago that would have given free passage to early Pleistocene explorers. Did Slater simply cite the wrong article? For reasons Russell didn't understand, he didn't think so.

The overhead lights blinked. With a start, Russell jumped from his chair and dashed for the stairs, slamming his head against the low ceiling of the stairway. He emerged dazed from the underworld. He felt his forehead to see if there was any blood. There was none.

"I hope you realize we've been here for 33 minutes," Sandra said, "and the press conference is scheduled to begin in four minutes. You better get cracking."

"Not four minutes," he said looking at his watch, "it begins in 64 minutes, at eleven."

"Not according to my information. There was a lot of email traffic about this press conference yesterday, parking restrictions, security, that sort of thing. It's scheduled to begin at ten, I'm certain."

But twice Wilde told me it starts at eleven, Russell recalled.

"I'm sure you're right, Sandra, but I hope you're wrong."

"Not a chance. While you were downstairs, I checked with the Campus Police. It now begins in three minutes," she said, looking at her watch.

"Thanks a lot for your help." He gave her a hug, and bolted for the doors shouting over his shoulder, "You're a love!"

"That's it?" she yelled back. "A hug after dragging me down here in the middle of the night?"

Russell pushed open the double doors and flew down the stairs headed for Batts Hall several buildings away.

"You still owe me a breakfast!" she yelled after him. Sandra stared at the doors for a few seconds, then turned off the lights and followed.

Chapter 16

Discovery of the Century

Russell arrived at Batts Hall perspiring heavily, even though the weather had turned cold and overcast. Four TV network trucks were parked out front with their antennae reaching to the heavens. No one was milling about the front of the building, not even the serial smokers, which meant the show had begun. Russell's watch read 10:03. President Dietz was noted for his punctuality, acquired from his years as chief engineer of the space program. Russell ran up the steps two at a time ready to somehow warn Wilde off any mention of a "Beringia uplift model."

Roper came running up behind him with Rider struggling to keep up. Rasping and panting for breath Rider barked, "You not only parked . . . your frigging truck . . . in a tow-a-way zone, he rasped, "you parked it in a disabled parking zone . . . next to a fire hydrant! We, you, could go to prison for that!"

"We'll worry about that after we've been on TV," Roper yelled, as he dashed into the entrance ahead of Rider.

Russell arrived first at the back of the auditorium and found the hall packed. He immediately saw that the event was meant to be a one-man show. On the stage two chairs were placed to the right of the podium, with Wilde in one and the other apparently just vacated by President Dietz, who stood behind the podium addressing the audience.

Suddenly, or perhaps not so suddenly, Russell could now see all the pieces falling into place: the secret CT scan of the hominid jaw; the invasion of Slater's site; the theft of what was meant to be Slater's discovery; and this pre-emptive press conference, which no doubt Wilde began planning the minute he left Presidio four days ago. All this was for the sole purpose of monopolizing Wilde's claim to "the discovery of the century," and, of course, deifying its alleged discoverer.

Beside Wilde was a table with a burnt orange cloth covering what had to be the skull. UT security guards stood on either side of the stage and TV cameras were positioned in the three aisles focused on the center of attention.

Russell edged his way along the outside wall to the right of the podium with others who were also standing, but not close enough for Wilde to see him. Russell had no intention of participating in any Q&A about Beringia or anything else.

Roper and Rider Harrington charged hell-bent down the center aisle. Since all the seats were taken, they just stood beside the stage next to the podium waving to the TV cameras.

Pots of poinsettias lined the stage blocking Wilde's view. When one of the cameras swung in his direction, Roper yanked off his cowboy hat and elbowed Rider to do the same. Two guards started to move toward them, but then thought better of it and let them be.

At that moment President Dietz was finishing up his introduction. "...so I proudly introduce to you a new and distinguished member of our faculty, a scholar of scholars, a man who throughout his remarkable career has added immensely to our knowledge of human origins. I am sure you will agree, however, that Professor Bert Wilde's latest find is the discovery of the century, one that begins a remarkable new chapter in our understanding of humankind. Ladies and gentleman, Professor Wilde!"

Wilde rose from his chair, shook hands with Dietz, and stepped behind the podium. Enthusiastic applause followed, but Wilde immediately raised his hands to quiet the crowd. He thanked President Dietz for his generous and insightful remarks.

The lights flooding the stage seemed to levitate Wilde's giant frame even higher than it was, as if he hovered before the audience.

A hush fell across the hall.

Seated on the front row directly in front of Wilde, and not more than ten feet from Roper and Rider, was the pugnacious and proud Dean Roberts, looking like he was about to witness the Second Coming—from the Rio Grande Valley.

Next to him sat Dean Cassie Burgess, who just remembered that Wilde had never sent her the memo she asked for summarizing the background of the discovery. She understood how busy he must have been over the last few days, but having his funding yanked by NSF, that was another matter, and disturbing. She made a mental note to make some discrete inquiries.

Sitting cozily at the end of the row was the PR

director, with a smile on his face, and a voluptuous strawberry blond, the latest acquisition for his PR team.

President Dietz stood off to one side brimming with pride and in anticipation of the national attention the university would receive. Unfortunately, Mrs. Wilde was nowhere to be seen. Nor would she be joining her husband that evening for a private showing of the skull held at a gathering of benefactors at President Dietz's home.

೮೦೮೦೮೦

Wilde looked slowly around the audience to give the impression that he was addressing each person individually. "If one of you happened to be in the recesses of the Congo basin and found a genuine 2,500-year-old Chinese temple, your discovery would prove no more surprising, indeed, no more shocking, than the one you are about to see. But my discovery was not made in Africa, or China, or Antarctica, but rather, it was made on more familiar terrain, which will, no doubt, generate extreme controversy and disbelief.

"This is as it should be, because great discoveries demand great scrutiny. Since this find has already been subjected to state-of-the-art laboratory analysis, however, I am confident that its significance will stand the test of time. With that said, let's not delay any longer."

Russell had to hand it to Wilde. He knew the right things to say, and God, did he have nerve. But he still couldn't understand how Slater could have been so wrong with his "pig" identification. And what about the "Beringia migration model"?

120

And the tragic death of Slater's fiancée? Is that somehow part of the equation? He'd ask Wilde about this at the first opportunity.

The audience buzzed with excitement as Wilde stepped to the table and stood behind it. As he did, the lights dimmed and a hush fell over the hall. He paused again looking over the audience, then slowly removed the cloth, reached down, and carefully raised the fossil for all to see.

At that moment, a giant image of the skull flashed on a screen behind the podium, its robust cheekbones, thick brow ridges, jutting face, and big-brained skull vault staring provocatively through eons of time.

"Ladies and gentleman!" Wilde boomed, "I introduce you to a fossil skull of a human ancestor that is one-and-a-half million years old, soon to be known around the world as *Homo americanus* . . . that was discovered in North America . . . in the Rio Grande Valley . . . in Presidio County . . . in THE GREAT STATE OF TEXAS!"

A collective gasp rippled through the audience. People in the audience caught their breath and looked at each other dumbfounded and uncomprehending. A one-and-a-half-million-year-old human from Texas? But in the next instant, the audience rose to their feet and exploded into applause and cheers. Wilde, again in his element, glowed. He had returned. He was not only back in the pantheon of science, he owned the temple!

After several minutes of clapping and cheering, the lights returned to normal and the skull faded into softer tones and disappeared. President Dietz stepped forward, beaming. The questions began even before he opened his mouth to begin the Q&A. One journalist after another shouted out to Professor Wilde:

"Professor, how did humans reach North America that long ago?"

"How can you be sure of its age?"

"Professor, why ancient humans in Texas?"

"Were other scientists with you?"

"Did you also find stone tools?"

"Yes, yes!" Dietz yelled, suddenly overwhelmed. "Professor Wilde will answer all of your questions one by one, but first, let's give the photographers and TV people a break so they can get close-ups of the skull and Professor Wilde!"

With that, TV cameramen and photographers began moving closer to the stage. Seeing his opportunity, Roper swept aside pots of poinsettias, sending them crashing to the floor as he leapt onto the stage. With Rider on his heels, he muscled his way past a security guard and stood beside Wilde posing for his TV fans.

Pandemonium erupted as journalists and photographers alike also charged onto the stage. More security guards joined the fray desperately trying to restrain the mob. Wilde momentarily recognized the two brothers, as he clutched the skull to his chest and backed up in the crush. He was besieged with more questions.

"How do you know the fossil's age?"

"How did ancient humans get to Texas?"

"How do you know its age?"

"How can you really know . . . ?"

Cameras flashed from all directions blinding Wilde as he turned from side to side like a bear taunted in a steel cage. Suddenly, someone in the jostling crowd slammed into Roper who stumbled backward. To keep from falling and being trampled, he reached out, grabbing Wilde's arm. As he did, the skull flew from Wilde's hands and crashed to the floor, shattering to pieces.

All movement suddenly came to a halt. Gasps echoed around him. Murmurs rippled across the hall. Then, as if on cue, those surrounding Wilde scrambled to pick up the pieces. Amid the turmoil, the horrified professor himself reached down and picked up a single fragment. Immediately, he recognized the smooth, pigment-colored interior and the tiny pits formed by air bubbles trapped in the dental plaster.

The skull was a fake.

Epilogue

At noon Christmas Day, Slater and Rocío loaded their belongings into his pickup after their week of exploration and camping at the Chase Ranch. They jumped into the truck and headed for the ranch owned by Rocío's Uncle Fernando on the other side of the Rio Grande, where the whole Benavides family was gathering for Christmas dinner and festivities. The river was dry, as it was in much of the valley, as the Border Patrol is all too aware.

"Now, Rocío, are you *sure* it's okay for me to be at your uncle's?"

"It's okay, I'm sure, if my uncle likes you."

"And if he doesn't?"

"That could be a *problema*."

"What do you mean, a *problema*? Doesn't he like Americans?"

"No, not really. A few."

"See, that's what I mean. I don't think this is a good idea."

"No, you don't see. The *problema* is whether I like you, and I haven't decided."

By then, Slater had nudged his truck up the bank on the Mexican side of the river.

 control

The story of "*Homo americanus*," or "Homo Fiasco," as the media dubbed the affair, was featured on the evening news from coast to coast. The event also made the front page of *The New York Times* the next morning:

> *Mr. Roper Harrington, a fourth generation rancher in Presidio County, Texas, whose Double-H Ranch contained the site of the alleged "American Man" skull, said during a televised interview that "I believed from the get-go that the professor planted that fake skull on the Double-H and then 'discovered it.' My family's been ranchin' that country for over a hundred years and there's nothin' there we ain't seen before, rode before, or tried to eat."*

The fraud, and of course, Wilde himself, would be the subject of intense investigations for months, even years, to come, led by a high-dollar team of criminal lawyers hired by the University of Texas. Unfortunately, President Eric Dietz lost his job. In his place, Cassie Burgess became the second woman president in the university's history.

From time to time, Slater read something about the scandal in the newspapers in Ciudad Chihuahua where he now lived. As it turned out, the jaw fragment that started the whole affair was real. The year before she died, Laura had bought it from a rogue antique dealer in Nairobi and had given it to her fiancée as a gift.

Author's Note

How could a paleoanthropologist as experienced as Wilde not recognize the Scorpion Arroyo skull as a forgery, a chimera blended from real and manufactured parts? Similarly, how did "Piltdown Man," recovered in Sussex, England in 1912, flummox the British scientific community for four decades, until it was revealed to be a monstrous hoax in 1953? The answer to these questions lies not only with the quality of the forgeries, made using increasingly sophisticated techniques, but in understanding the motives of the *victims*.

Acknowledgments

My gratitude goes to those laboratories, departments, and libraries of the University of Texas at Austin mentioned in this story, and to the Writer's League of Texas for technical support. For comments on the manuscript, my thanks go to Clifford Jolly, Claud Bramlett, Tom Doyal, Dean Falk, Joe Nick Patrosky, Don Webb, Linda Maraniss, Pat Foss, Joan Neubauer, Mindy Reed, Jim and Jane White, and especially to my wife, Judy.

CPSIA information can be obtained at www.ICGtesting.com
Printed in the USA
LVOW07s1124170815

450403LV00001B/4/P